MAN
CARD

SARINA BOWEN & TANYA EBY

RENNIE ROAD BOOKS

1 MANIACAL LAUGH

Ash

Before getting out of my car, I slip into incognito mode—I tug my blonde hair into a sleek ponytail, pull on my black leather gloves, and lower my shades.

There. Now I'm ready for action.

I'm dressed in skintight black jeans, a black cashmere turtleneck with a sweet cowl neckline and black ankle boots. It's the perfect cat burglar outfit, while also totally appropriate for cocktails later with my besties, Brynn and Sadie.

Do I have an outfit for everything, or what? It's my superpower.

Closing the car door with a quiet click, I turn to survey the mansion. It's gorgeous—a show home on Reed's Lake. I'm not here to actually steal anything from the homeowner. I'm just here to claim what's rightfully mine—a big, fat commission for selling this house.

If I get that commission, I'm one step closer to winning the year-end bonus at work. Furthermore, I'll have outdone my competitor Braht. The world's most irritating man.

Victory is going to be so sweet.

Ignoring the wrought-iron gates, I sneak through a hole in the boxwood hedge. It's broad daylight, so anyone could see me. But if I stay close to the hedge and hunch over a bit, maybe I'll be invisible.

It's not rational, I know that, but I'm not feeling super rational these days.

The problem is Braht. He brings out all my craziest behavior. I've had to put up with him far too often this month as we try to coordinate the sale of this home. It's all the more reason why I deserve the commission on this house, and he deserves to rub my feet.

I pause because something happens to me when I think of Braht rubbing my feet. What is that peculiar feeling?

Goddammit! It's a throb! The image of his long, manicured fingers on my instep just makes my loins throb.

Motherfucker.

All the more reason to focus.

I have made it past the perfectly trimmed bushes, and I'm now standing at the giant entrance to the home. It's a beautiful property that Tom Spanner, my bestie's boyfriend, owns. He's selling it so he and Brynn can live in a smaller house on a bigger lake, where they'll be disgustingly happy together.

That's all well and good, but I can't fathom why they had to force Braht and me to work together on this sale. It means I actually have to answer his calls. Just thinking about it steams me up. It's been a few days since my last yoga class, too.

Deep breaths. Deep breaths.

I reach out with my black gloved hands and commence Operation Suck It, Braht.

The goal: lock him out of the house right before his scheduled showing. I'm changing all the codes on the lockboxes. And then I'll stick around to watch him squirm. He deserves to squirm a little, if only because he's the kind of guy who wears khaki shorts and a pink button-down in October.

But, hey. It's not like I've been checking him out whenever

we're here at the house together. It's not like I keep noticing his surprisingly muscular legs, or the perpetually tan V of skin on his tight chest...

Fuck. Distraction is dangerous for cat burglars!

So I redirect my focus to the lockboxes, punching in the numbers, performing a little technical voodoo. And...voila! New codes.

Now I feel a new kind of tingle as I picture his face the moment he realizes he's been had. He'll fumble then, disappointing his buyers when he can't get into the house. They'd have to have to use pogo sticks to peek into the upstairs windows.

And no one buys a house they can't inspect. Not even rich people.

Feeling vindicated, I run back to my car. My heart thuds with excitement, and another emotion, too. I feel...nefarious. And it's great! Okay, technically it's bad. But being bad can be exquisite.

In my reckless youth, I let my inner bad girl out more often. It didn't work out so well, so these days I keep myself on a much tighter leash. But today I can feel her rattling her chain.

I slip into my car and check my vantage point. I'm parked under a beautiful willow tree, where I'll wait until poor little Brahtie shows up, and I win. The end.

———

Okay, I've been sitting here for three minutes. Three minutes is the entire time I can be evil before I just get bored. Why is he late? Uggghh.

And because I need to be stealthy and watchful, I can't even listen to music or distract myself by checking my phone. So I'm forced to just sit here and analyze my entire life.

And, let's face it, my past is like a dark alley I try to stay clear of.

My teen years provided plenty of cringeworthy moments, but those errors were mostly unimportant, like wearing a white T-shirt while canoeing with the football team. I forgive myself for little things like this.

But my grownup regrets are harder to excuse. The first one is a man named Dwight Engersoll. I can't think too hard about it because it makes me anxious. But suffice it to say Dwight is now safely far away from me. Locked far away. Literally. In the Michigan State Penitentiary.

My second regret? It's much less traumatic, but I was equally stupid and vulnerable. It involved a pantry, nudity, being coated with flour, and the most mind-blowing orgasm I've ever experienced. An orgasm so intense that not only did my toes curl, but they actually cramped.

It was sort of a good cramp, but still. A cramp. I probably shouldn't regret that sexual experience, because who can actually regret an orgasm that makes you glow? But let me tell you, it was regrettable anyway. First, because the sound of said orgasm was caught and broadcast to ten thousand subscribers on Brynn's new cooking show, and secondly because I was doing it...with Braht.

Braht!

Just the sound of his name makes my toes curl. Wait. Not in the good post-orgasm way, but in the bad I-hate-him-so-much-I-could-spit way. It's hard to explain why, since he's rich, witty and scrumptiously attractive. But if you met him, you'd understand. He's tall and lanky with floppy golden hair that falls into his face. He wears a shit-eating grin most of the time, along with clothing that's always, *always* in pastel colors.

He's like the reincarnation of James Spader in the eighties, complete with his collar up. He manscapes, gets manicures, and I'm pretty sure he mansplains with the best of them, but when we're in the same room, the hairs on my arms rise. Also, my nipples harden.

And I am *not* hitting that again. No ma'am. Nope. Never again. There will be no nipple hardening here. Nipple hardening leads to my brain shutting down, which is often followed by PLC. Poor Life Choices.

Clearly, I cannot afford any more PLC. I'm still picking up the pieces of my life that Dwight destroyed. I was attracted to him, too.

God, I'm really an idiot.

Now Braht is ten minutes late. Ten! It isn't like him. Not that I pay much attention, but a guy who matches his alligator shirts to his socks is rarely the type to be late.

Maybe his clients aren't interested after all.

I find myself strangely disappointed by this idea, even though I want the sale all to myself. Then again, if he doesn't show up, I don't get the satisfaction of watching him squirm. And, ohhhhhhh, I want to see him squirm.

I hunker down, and check my phone, which I've wired up to show me the feed from the mansion's front door. Nothing yet and then, finally...!

The wrought-iron gate swings open! And there he is!

He's driving a station wagon that's a...convertible? A wood-paneled station wagon convertible, circa 1977. What is WRONG with this man? There's a couple in the car with him, and they're all laughing gaily together.

Though not for long, right?

He pulls into the driveway, turns off the car, and a smile slowly spreads across my face. My nipples are hard, but they'll calm down. Braht has no idea what's in store for him. I laugh a little, maniacally, because *come on*. When you have the opportunity for a maniacal laugh, you take it.

I start the stopwatch feature on my phone and wait.

Sixty seconds: no sign of the station wagon's departure, but they're probably chatting on the front steps.

Two minutes: Nothing. No panicky texts. I know they'll start rolling in any minute.

Four minutes: Hmm. He probably decided to show the grounds first. Our friend Tom is a master gardener along with being a kickass builder. He did the most incredible landscaping. It's droolworthy.

Ten minutes: Okay, there aren't that many shrubberies to ogle. Any second now, Braht will realize I've burned him. Burrrrrn!

Fifteen minutes: The house has three entrances. He's obviously trying his code on all of them. Repeatedly.

Twenty minutes: OH KILL ME ALREADY HOW LONG DOES A GIRL HAVE TO WAIT TO CLAIM SWEET VICTORY?

A long time, it seems.

Eventually, the suspense proves too much for me. Since I'm still wearing the best cat burglar outfit ever (with sparkly black round-toed ankle boots. Did I mention the shoes?), I quietly open my car door and get out to investigate.

As I creep toward the gate again, the willow tree and the fabulous boxwood hedge provide just the right amount of cover. I can't let him spot me, not until his buyers give up and leave, and I can emerge as the winner.

Peeking around the hedge, I see the station wagon, parked at a jaunty angle on the white pebbled circular drive. I can't risk those pebbles, they'll crunch underfoot. So I stick to the grass, crouching down and bolting across the lawn toward the exterior wall of the house. I'm there in a flash.

Seriously, I'm acing this. It deserves an achievement sticker in my planner. Since I don't have any stickers for being stealthy, I'll probably just go with a cute running shoe sticker. But first, more recon.

Crouching under a dining room window, I listen for voices. And I hear one! It's...Ella Fitzgerald. Coming from inside the house!

But that can't be right. The place was quiet a half hour ago.

There are really two possibilities. Maybe the ghost of Ella haunts Tom's mansion. Although there was no mention of ghosts on his disclosure form. Or, worse, someone has made it inside that house and is now playing music.

Fuck. It's possible I've been outwitted. It's rare these days, but no one is infallible.

I need to stand up straight and look inside, because A) I need to know if I've been beaten and B) my thighs are burning from crouching beside this window.

Slowly, I raise my head until I can see over the sill, and what I see inside floods me with anger. Braht and the laughing couple are still laughing. But they're doing it seated around Tom's gleaming dining table. Worse, there's a silver tea service on a shining tray, and they're all holding Noritake teacups in one hand and finger sandwiches in the other.

Finger sandwiches!

Tea!

Noritake!

My stomach growls. Or maybe that was just a regular, angry growl. He's having a fucking *tea party* in there. I'm going to kill him dead.

Somehow my anger announces my presence. The next thing I know, Braht has locked gazes with me. And he *smiles*.

My blood pressure doubles as he gets up, gallops around the table and cranks the window open. "Why, Ashley! What are you doing out there in Tom's chrysanthemum bed?"

"I'm..." My panic only lasts a nanosecond, and the part of my psyche that's willing to beat Braht at any cost comes roaring back, and I realize I need to double down on my deception. "The lockbox combination isn't working. What did you do?"

His smile only widens. "Come around to the front, honey bear. I'll let you in."

Having no choice, I stomp out of the mums in my killer boots and around to the front door.

Braht

I swallow a bite of the most delectable cucumber and smoked salmon sandwich as I dance toward the front door. Life is good.

I have quality tunes on Tom's sound system, and gourmet snacks.

And, I'll be honest, I'm totally turned on right now. Ash brings out the beast in me when we compete. I have to hand it to her. She's proving herself to be a formidable opponent. The lockbox trick was a good effort.

Unfortunately for her, I anticipated this maneuver and wore shorts to work today. After a quick apology for the delay, I left my clients to enjoy the lake view from Tom's exquisite patio while I waded out beside the dock to the *fourth* lockbox on the boathouse door.

The one that Ashley missed.

Then I jogged down the boathouse stairs, into the tunnel connecting it to the main house, put on the kettle for tea, arranged my nom noms on a tray, and then invited my clients into Tom's home for a tea party.

I have cookies for dessert. The whole thing is a piece of cake, really. They don't call me The Closer for nothing.

When I swing open the front door, Ash is standing on the front porch looking fabulous—all long legs and cashmere-wrapped tits and perfect cheekbones. With a defiant look on her face that always makes me hard.

Oh, Ash. You have no idea what you do to me.

Every time I see her I'm wrecked, right from *hello*. This has been going on for years. But lately it's gotten even worse, ever since Ash jumped me and I got a taste of just how good we are together.

As always, it takes me a second to push through the familiar feeling of being karate chopped by Cupid. "Nice outfit, Ashleykins," I manage to snap. "But those jeans are snug, baby girl. It's a great look, but how am I going to get them off you later when it's time to bend you over the sideboard and have my filthy way with you?"

There's a long pause and I think she's actually considering it. Then Ashley gasps, and her cheeks redden further. "You cannot say things like that! We're at *work*. Have you read the employee handbook? Does the term 'hostile work environment' ring any bells?"

This should be a perfectly valid point, and I have always respected a woman's right to be the mistress of her own domain. Except for one little flaw in her argument. "Ashleycakes, the first time we ever had a conversation about this house, you ended it by unzipping my fly and swallowing my dick in Brynn's pantry."

Now the blush is creeping down her neck, and right into that delectable cleavage. I'm actually a little worried about spontaneous combustion. Good thing Tom showed me where he keeps the fire extinguisher in the coat closet. Safety first.

"We're not in the pantry now," she grinds out.

"Pity. That thing you do with your tongue really rocks my world."

That's when her head pops off and bounces down the brick portico stairs. Okay, not really. But the look on her face makes this seem possible.

"Stop. It." She takes a deep breath. "Business, Braht. We need to talk business."

"Fab," I agree. "So let's talk about three lockboxes that don't work and a fourth one that requires water entry. I don't suppose you have a set of waders in that cute little car you hid up the block?"

"Water entry?"

"The boathouse. You don't think I descended from the chimney, do you? I'm good, but I'm not that good."

Her perfect pink tongue appears in the corner of her mouth and her eyes go a little soft-focus. She's remembering just how good I am with my hands. And my tongue.

I snap my fingers. "Focus, baby. Why don't you work on this lockbox thing. Any idea how we can undo the damage?"

"Uh..." She shakes herself. "It must have been a miscommunication with...my intern."

"Your intern?" What the actual fuck. Realtors don't have interns.

But Ash is nodding rapidly. "Her name is Zelda. She's young and inexperienced. She must have, uh, mistyped the codes I sent her. I'll get her to fix it and then I'll send you the new codes."

Intern *my ass*. "Zelda, huh? Is she my type, too?"

"What do you mean, *too?* I am not your type, Braht."

"You are the walking definition of my type, Ash." I didn't mean to say it so forcefully, but it's just true. "And you don't need to tell me about Zelda, because I'm sure I'll meet her myself tomorrow."

"Tomorrow?" Ash blinks, as if maybe there's an appointment she's forgotten.

"Tomorrow," I confirm. Then I drop the bomb I've been waiting to drop on her since I got the news three days ago. I needed to do it in person, because her reaction is going to be epic. "I've been transferred to your branch. We're going to be *office buddies*." I waggle my brows. It's a thing I do. It's a thing I do around Ash because it makes her squirm. And I love to make her squirm.

She sucks in a breath. "My...branch?" The look on her face is one I see often when she looks at me—an intriguing blend of lust mixed with horror. "You don't mean...my branch of the company. At my...physical location."

"Yes indeed! I asked Bill to put our desks near each other, too. Because we're working on this deal together. Corporate asked me to help get the revenue up at the Eastown branch. We're going to be the power couple of Ernst VanderMollen Realty."

"But...!" Her pretty face drains of color. She's almost paler than the golden highlights in her hair. "You can't do that! I've made Top Salesperson nine months out of the last twelve!"

Well, ouch. I hadn't thought of that. "Sorry, honey bear. You're going to have to share that trophy occasionally. It will be good for morale. The other kids need to see that success has more than one face."

"You're...this is a joke, right?" she whispers. "Good one, Braht. Well played."

"It's all too real, Ash. We're colleagues now. Once the shock wears off, I'm sure you'll remember how much you like me."

"I do not. Like you," she says, crossing her arms firmly.

"Then why do your nipples get so pointy whenever we speak?"

Ash lets out a shriek of indignation, and I have to duck as she takes a swing at me.

2 BRAIN FREEZE AND SCREAMING ORGASMS

Ash

"How many am I up to?" I ask, pulling the next frozen daiquiri toward me on the bar.

"That's your second drink, you lush," Brynn says and then does a little giggle-burp thing.

Though for me, two drinks is kind of a lot. I *feel* drunk. Actually, I felt dazed before I even sat down on this bar stool. Drunk with disbelief. Now I'm drunk with disbelief and brain freeze. "Braht and I cannot share an office," I say for the tenth time at least.

"You can share a pantry though," Sadie says with a smirk.

I do not deign to acknowledge that comment.

"You're the one who's always telling us to *suck it up, buttercup*," Brynn points out. "Tomorrow this will seem more manageable. You're just in shock right now."

"It's time to self-soothe," Sadie adds. "The daiquiris are a good start. A home facial and a little online shopping later will have you feeling like new."

"Is that your professional opinion?"

"For you, yes. If I were giving advice to Brynn that she needed to self-soothe, I'd tell her to take a running leap at her mister handy so they could cover each other in chocolate and then lick it off."

Sadie totally has my number. So does Brynn. They're like the only two people on the planet I can totally relax with. That's why I can admit anything to them. "There isn't really a Zelda," I hiccup into my drink. "I invented her on the fly."

"We got that, hon," Sadie says. "Clearly you have to fire her before tomorrow morning. Poor Zelda. Such a brief stint in the world of real estate. I had such high hopes for her."

"Or she could take a leave of absence," Brynn suggests. "Zelda came down with shingles and needs her rest!"

I groan into my drink. "Nobody will believe that."

"Shingles really hurt," Brynn says, trying to convince me.

"It's not the shingles part I have a problem with. It's that... dammit...Braht is too smart to fall for my bullshit."

"Too smart, huh?" Sadie asks, trying to cover a smile. "That's the first nice thing you've ever said about him."

"Not the first," I correct her. "He's good at giving screaming orgasms." Not that I'm ever having another one with him or anyone else. I'm through with men.

"I need a screaming orgasm," Sadie sighs.

"Coming right up!" the bartender says as he passes by.

"Wait!" Sadie says, "I meant..."

But he's already talking to someone else farther down the bar.

"I think you have a kink for fake people," Brynn says.

"What?" I take another deep drink of the frozen goodness in my glass. It's freezing my brain in a good way.

"Zelda isn't your first fake person," she points out. "There's also Hunter. The fake boyfriend."

"That's different," I grumble. But it isn't really. Both Hunter and Zelda came to me in my hour of need, the way real people often don't. Present company excepted.

"Are your parents still buying it?" Sadie asks. "How long have you and Hunter been a couple?"

"Um..." I do the math. "Over a year now. We're going to have to break up soon because the holidays are coming. I like the holidays too much to skip them."

"You mean..." Brynn's eyes cross a little bit because she's thinking hard. "If you were having Christmas Eve with Hunter's folks, you'd have to be absent from your own parents' place?"

"Exactly. Last year Hunter and I were too new to spend the holidays together. But my parents are going to expect him to turn up. Or worse—if I pretend to go to his folks' place, I'll end up sitting home alone. And that's just wrong. I can't give up Christmas Eve, not even for Hunter."

"...Who is *fake*," Sadie reminds me.

"Right. Of course," I blather. "But we're talking eggnog here, and that is serious shit." Once in a while I do almost forget that Hunter isn't real. Last month Hunter sent flowers to my office because I was feeling kind of low, and it's weird to send yourself flowers.

Ask me how I know.

"But if you have to break up with him," Sadie muses, "then what was the point?"

"The point was appeasing my parents." *Duh.* "It's been months since they've dropped all those terrible hints about what it might be like if I become a cat lady and die alone. Even if I break up with my imaginary boyfriend, at least I can show them I tried."

"You didn't, though," Sadie points out. "You *faked* trying."

"Are you going to charge me for this hour?" I snark at Sadie, who is a therapist. Her office has a couch to lie on and everything. It's the real deal.

"Maybe your parents were right to worry," she presses. "They think your ability to trust men was irrevocably harmed by Dwi..."

"HEY!" I yell before she can get the word out. "We do not say his name aloud. Especially not tonight." I'm not even joking about this. There's a pain in my chest when I think about him. It's real, and it's scary.

Sadie rolls her eyes and I feel better suddenly. "Okay. Fine.

You're a perfectly healthy person with two invisible friends. Nothing weird about it."

"Wait," Brynn says, a hand on her heart. "I *am* real, right? Ash didn't invent me? Is this real life?" She fakes a swoon.

But Sadie grabs her boob and makes the sound of a car horn. Twice. It's nice to see her being a goofball. "Totally real, sweetie," she says. "You can't honk the boob of an imaginary friend."

"Whew." Brynn wipes fake sweat off her brow. "For a moment there I was filled with doubt."

"Here's your screaming orgasm," the bartender says, plunking a glass in front of Sadie.

We all burst out laughing. Then we unwrap three straws and each of us has a taste. "Not bad," Brynn says. "But the real thing is better."

"You're the only one having them," Sadie points out. "The rest of us have to make do."

Brynn and I exchange a glance. Sadie keeps hinting that things aren't going well in her marriage, but when we try to pry some details out of her, she always clams up.

Maybe tonight I have a way to ease her into talking about it. "You guys, the Michigan Association of Realtors published their Best and Worst lists today. That's always good for a chuckle."

"Did we win Worst Winter Weather again?" Brynn asks.

"Nope." Although I wouldn't be surprised. "But get this—our county is the most happily married in the entire nation."

"Bullshit," Sadie snorts.

Brynn and I exchange another glance.

"There's got to be some bias in those figures," Sadie insists. "I'll buy that people tend to *stay* married around here, but that's just pressure from the church pastor. And look at us. Brynn is very happily *unmarried*. And both of you are divorced. So if we live in the most happily married place in the land, we are bringing down the average. Hard." She punctuates this with a slurp of the screaming orgasm.

"What else is this area known for?" Brynn asks. "There has to be something. Best healthcare? Most musical? Awesome Mexican food?"

Not quite. "Cheap parking," I say with a sigh.

"Cheap. Parking," Sadie repeats slowly. "That is really not doing it for me tonight."

I'm just about to agree with her when my phone flashes and trills.

"Sorry," I say and grab it, struggling to make the thing shut up. I read the text even though I don't want to. And of course it's Braht.

Braht: **Hey girl! Nice desk accessories! Somebody likes pens a lot. Long, thick pens.**

Grrr! Braht is at my desk? **Don't touch my pens. They're from Japan. I count them every night before I leave.** Everyone in the office knows not to touch my shit. One time a trainee used my Korean washi tape to hang up a poster and I made him buy me a new roll. The shipping charges alone cost more than his lunch. That lesson was not soon forgotten.

But they're smooth and silky just like you, Ash. Nice paper, too. Hey—I have a favor to ask. It's about tomorrow.

Get. Away. From my desk. I feel violated picturing Braht touching all my things with those long, artistic fingers of his. From five miles away I can feel his boyish grin as he taunts me. His Ralph-Lauren-model face, smirking...

"Are you okay, Ash?" Brynn asks. "You look a little flushed."

"I'm fine," I snap. "One sec." There is a text bubble on the screen, so Braht is typing another stupid message. Whatever favor he asks of me, it's an automatic no. My finger hovers over the N key in preparation.

Can you show the house tomorrow at two? he asks.

That is a strange request, and it throws me for a half second. But then I'm filled with indignation faster than you can say *bitch mode*. **What if I'm busy at two?** I fire back. Does he really expect me to show the house to *his* clients? Then I have a better idea. **If I show the house, it's my sale**.

Wow, territorial much? he asks. **Fine, cutie. It's your client. The couple's name is Mr. and Mrs. Robert VanHeimlich. Two o'clock sharp. You're up, sweet cheeks.**

...

...

I can be up, too. Any time you want.

Fucking Braht and his never-ending nicknames for me. I'm 5'9 and I work hard to be sleek and ice cold. There is no way anyone on this planet looks at me and can think I look like an "Ashley Poo" or "Sweet cheeks" or whatever. I'm Ash Power. I'm always Ash Power. I will always be...

"Why are you giggling?" asks Brynn.

"I'm not sure I'd call that a giggle," says Sadie, sounding afraid. "It's really close to an evil laugh."

Then I realize I am almost maniacally laughing. Again.

And my nipples!

GODDAMMIT!

"I'm fine," I say, texting one last time. **I'll do it. 2pm. Gotta run now.** Then I shut off my phone. "Ack. It's just Braht giving me a client, which is really fucking strange."

"Why?" Sadie asks.

"We don't just give each other clients! That's not how it is with us."

Brynn lifts an eyebrow. "How is it, then?"

"We hate each other! We flirt and then destroy each other. And this couple—Mr. and Mrs. VanHeimlich. Do you think they could be part of *those* VanHeimlichs?" The VanHeimlich family owns the world's largest bible publishing company, and they own half of Grand Rapids. They're a force in the community. Nobody really likes them, but their money sure is nice.

Both Brynn and Sadie are blinking at me now. "That's exactly the sort of people who could afford Tom's house," Brynn points out. "This could be great!"

Still, I don't trust it. "Braht's no dummy. If this was a great client, he'd never just hand them to me. He said he's busy at two tomorrow. Too busy to make a sale?"

"You just said something nice about Braht," Sadie points out.

"No I didn't!" What a crazy idea.

"You said, and I quote, 'Braht's no dummy.'" Sadie smirks.

"Oh, please. Faint praise at best. And I never said he was stupid. I only said he's an asshole who cares more about his manicure and golf swing than hard work. He's Mr. Entitled." I shudder. "Just like a man."

"Then why do you get all breathless and weird when you talk about him?" Sadie asks, slurping the last of her screaming orgasm. For a moment I'm distracted by a slurping screaming orgasm. Whatever. *Focus, Ash!*

"I don't get breathless," I yelp, sorta breathy. God. It's obviously time to call it a night. "I'll see you two later, okay? I've got research to do before tomorrow's showing."

Over their protests, I give Brynn and Sadie each a peck and scoot out of the bar. I need to go home and do a deep dive into the VanHeimlich family tree, so I know what I'm dealing with. They could be cousins of the CEO. It's a big Dutch family. This part of Michigan has a huge population of Dutch people. I make a mental note to point out Tom's tulips.

I've got this. I can feel it in my belly. I'm going to sell this house and crush Braht and his glorious pecs with my bare hands.

I mean, crush *Braht*. Just Braht. Nothing about his pecs or my bare hands on those pecs, or...drifting downward.

My brain hates me. It loves to remember Braht's smooth skin and taut body and those few minutes in the pantry when he...

Stop it, brain.

I have a house to sell.

3 UNVEILING THE HUMAN FORM

Braht

"You ready, Bramly?" I call to my younger brother.

He does not look the least bit ready. He's hanging out on my couch in his underwear playing Destiny 2.

"Don't you have your own place for that? And put a towel down!" One shouldn't sweat on Italian leather.

"Seriously?" he says and gestures to my living room, which is, I admit, not organized and piled high with my stuff. My important stuff.

"It's Italian," I whine, because this is enough of an explanation.

He groans, rolls his eyes and says, "Okay, *Dad*" in that half-kidding-but-not-really way he's been saying since he was twelve and I, well, actually took over raising him. Long story.

"I'm on a schedule here!" I say. "If we're going to pull off this epic mission, then we need to get moving as quickly as possible." To show him how very serious I am I start to unbutton my shirt.

Bramly tosses the controller onto the table and lets out a dramatic sigh. "Hold up! I'm not ready to see my brother naked yet. I have to channel my muse."

His muse. And people think I'm the ridiculous one.

Bramly slips into his artist's mojo by donning one of our grandpa's old shirts from the 60s, but no pants. Maybe that's why the shirt has so many pockets. He tops this off with a beret, and I've never been sure whether he wears that thing ironically or not. Then he grabs his camera and takes a slow, focusing breath. He stops being frat boy Bramly and becomes serious Bramly. It's actually a cool process that I am completely down with.

I'm a live-and-let-live kind of guy. Don't let the designer clothes fool you.

Bramly is not like me, though. He fancies himself an artistic photographer. He's been after me to model some shots for him that he can include in his upcoming show. He likes to Explore the Human Form. I'm pretty sure Exploring the Human Form means naked people in good lighting.

I'm totally fine with that, too. I've been manscaping for years and it feels like all that hard work will finally pay off.

Okay, to be fair, this *is* a little odd. I never considered modeling (mostly) naked for my kid brother until now. What can I say? Ash brings out the best in me. Actually, Ash brings out the *beast* in me—and I can already feel him rising. *Down, boy.*

Bramly motions to me and I follow him into my home office, which has been totally transformed. He's pretty much gutted the room and now there's a velvet settee and all these round lighting fixtures. It actually looks like an artist's studio. He's adjusting his camera and his beret, so it's obviously showtime.

We have just twelve hours to get these photos shot and printed, which should be barely enough time. I'll also need to install a hidden camera in Tom's house. Or maybe two. I don't want to miss anything. And, sure, this won't help to sell the house, but that's okay. I'm not trying to prevent Ash from selling it, I just want to make her work for it.

The way she's made me work for everything over the past few years.

Good thing I've always loved a challenge, and Ash is the biggest challenge I've ever encountered.

"You're already thinking of her, aren't you?" Bramly says.

"How do you...?" I look down. Ah.

Bramly snaps his fingers. "On the settee. Now! I'm emotionally and spiritually prepared to turn you into art! Quick, before you lose your...inspiration."

I lie back on the velvet, which is soft against my skin. It's...stimulating.

"Tighten your abs," my brother barks. "Drape one hand onto your chest. Yes! Like that." I hear the shutter clicking away. "Good! Look over my right shoulder and think of...whatever it is you like about women."

I laugh, and smirk at the camera, and I tug the hem of my boxers down just a little bit. Ash is going to love me for this. Or hate me.

Same dif.

Ash

By two o'clock the following day, I'm standing on the porch of Tom's house in a knee-length plaid skirt and a starched white blouse. And pearls, goddammit. I had to dig to the bottom of my jewelry box to find them.

Totally worth it.

Last night I took seven pages of notes in my bullet journal about the client. (And earned a research sticker—a cute little magnifying glass!) The VanHeimlich clan are Dutch-American multi-millionaires. They set up some kind of pyramid scheme to sell bibles and breakfast mixes or something. They're super conservative, subscribe to "traditional gender roles" (hence the unflattering skirt.) And they donated a whack ton of money to fund a museum that walks you through how the earth is flat and Darwin was wrong. No lie.

I can work with this, even if it makes my sphincter clench a little.

It's not about me, though. I'm a realtor, so it's about them. Their needs. I am here to prove that their needs include Tom's house and all its expensive, impenetrable surfaces. I'm here for them. Also for the fat commission.

In service to this higher goal, I'm even wearing sensible shoes. All of it makes me chafe, but that's okay. I can do this.

I have one moment of panic when their car pulls in right behind mine. Usually I like to open up the house ahead of the client's arrival. The VanHeimlichs are early.

No problem! I won't let my irritation show. When they step out of the car, I'm all smiles. Mrs. VanHeimlich is wearing a high-collared blouse and several diamonds on her pale fingers. After my warmest possible greeting, I turn to unlock Tom's door. I am a tiny bit nervous that the doors won't open, or they'll be wired in such a way as to give me an electrical shock, but nothing like that happens.

"Watch your step!" I sing as I enter the darkened foyer. "And welcome to your new home!" There is a slight delay while I feel around for the light switch. Was it always this dark in here? I bump into a console table. *Awkward!* But then my hand finds the switch and I turn it on.

Whew! I've opened my mouth to apologize when I just happen to notice there's a framed photo on the console table that wasn't there yesterday. It's...holy shit. It's a photo of a man's chiseled chest, the model pulling down on his boxer briefs just to the point where there's a nice bit of neatly trimmed hair, and a bulge in his underpants THAT I RECOGNIZE.

I recognize the shape, because I had it in my mouth once.

A little squeak of shock escapes me before I can rein it in. And I slam that photo down on the console with a bang.

"Everything okay, dear?" Mr. VanHeimlich asks.

"That wasn't a bug, was it?" his wife gasps.

"No!" I protest, my voice all high and crazy. "Just clumsy. Knocked it down. Come right this way!" I babble.

I want to kill him. I think I would do it, too, if it didn't mean a prison sentence. I have to stay out of the prison system so I don't bump into my ex.

Moving on.

My anxiety notches up again as I lead my clients into the kitchen. "Lovely light in here!" I say, my gaze skittish. "Great space for entertaining!"

There are several new objects in the kitchen, damn it. But they're subtle. There's a bunch of long, firm bananas hanging from a hook. Those weren't there yesterday. There's also a platter of carefully arranged eggplants on a tray. They're shiny and bulbous and I choke back a giggle at the sight of them.

I hope the VanHeimlichs aren't very well versed in emoji humor. But, heck, something tells me they're not.

This is fine, I coach myself. *We've still got this under control.*

"How many square feet of interior living space is there?" Mr. VanHeimlich asks.

"Four thousand!" I bleat, gesturing to the staircase like a demented gameshow host. "And a generous basement, leading to the boathouse!" I position my body in front of the eggplants. From my vantage point I can see the dining table, where a vase of voluptuous orchids has appeared. They are glistening and peachy pink. Like female genitalia.

I'm going to maim him. I wonder what the sentencing guidelines say about maiming?

My gaze swings in the other direction, and I'm wondering if I shouldn't lead the VanHeimlichs out the back way, toward the porch. But there's a suspicious pile of magazines visible by the door, and I'm terrified to learn what's on their covers.

The dining room it is, then. "Step right this way," I say, my sensible pumps clicking on the flooring tiles. The VanHeimlichs are right on my heels as I throw on the switch for the ultramodern chandelier.

Mrs. VanHeimlich gasps. I know the place is beautiful, but come on, that's a little dramatic.

Then Mr. VanHeimlich mutters "Dear God, it's an abomination!" I know something is very wrong when he whips off his jacket and tosses it over his wife's head. That would make sense if the room were filled with bats and he was trying to protect his wife. I mean, bats burrow into hair, I'm pretty sure.

There aren't any bats though. The dining room looks totally gorgeous. It's all glass and marble and giant framed art posters.

Wait a minute.

Every poster has been replaced with a portrait of...Braht. I gasp too, but damn if I'm going to let Mr. VanHeimlich cover my eyes with a jacket because I want to keep looking and looking and looking at...

At...

"Holy hell," I breathe and do a 360. There must be six different poses, each one sexier than the next. Beautiful, chiseled, hairless Braht in a variety of sexy, bulging poses.

But it's the one of him stroking himself on the velvet settee that makes me pass out.

Literally.

4 GOING ALL OUTLANDER

Braht

Thanks to modern security technology, I see my girl go down like a brick wall, right there on Tom's dining room floor.

And what does that dickhead VanHeimlich do? He *steps over her* and leads his wife out. I'm speechless, although I'll be giving him a piece of my mind later. Just not yet. I'm running out the back door of my house, leaping over Mrs. VanDanbunk's lilac hedge and running toward Tom's place. It's only a quarter mile away, because it was me that convinced Tom to buy a place in the same posh neighborhood where Casa Braht is located. I've gone the back way, which means I'm setting off motion-detecting lights and sensors like crazy, but I don't care.

Because Ash.

Good thing I ran track in high school, before I discovered golf.

I'm there in a flash, racing through his yard to the walkway in back, then pound around to the front. Vaulting up the stairs I arrive in the dining room just as Ash is struggling to sit up.

"Oh, fuck," she says, rubbing the back of her head. "I don't think I made the sale." Her eyes seem to come into focus. Then her gaze rakes up my body, from my legs to my, well, most excellent bits. Then up to my face. She frowns. "This is your fault."

I squat down beside her. "Yeah, it is. I didn't expect you to react quite that dramatically. I'm flattered, though."

"You absolute dick." Her beautiful eyes narrow. "I could have sold this house! You robbed me. You robbed us *both?* Who does that?"

"They weren't going to buy it."

"You don't know that!" she yells.

Except I do. "They have a similarly sized home just a half mile away that they're trying to sell so they can move to Bermuda. Theirs is priced too high, so their realtor suggested they stop in and do a comparison."

"Fuck!" Ash says, sounding even grumpier. "You set me up for no reason?"

"For fun," I say, feeling sorry. "Those VanHeimlichs are assholes, baby. I wanted to shock them. I should have let you in on the joke. I, uh..." It wasn't easy to get my mouth to make the words. "I'm sorry. Truly."

Ash's face softens the moment I say it. *Note to self: Ash appreciates a good apology.*

She still looks a little woozy, though, and my ego isn't big enough to assume it's because of my hotness. Well, not *all* because of my hotness. "You might have a bump on your head. Let me help you up." I grasp her under the arms and lift her right to her feet.

"Oh," she says softly. "Thank you." I keep an arm behind her back, because she's still a little unsteady. Her eyes wander to the largest poster, the one of me on the settee. It's a masterwork, if I'm honest. Everybody, no matter how humble, likes to look his best. (Not that I'm humble. What's the point of that?)

And Bramly really delivered the goods on these photos. Looking your best is 70% confidence, 20% raw material, 10% imported photographic lenses and 5% lighting. Pay no mind to the total of more than 100%, because in my case that's what you're getting. The poster is 105% awesome.

Ash's eyes roam the photo, and she sort of sags against me.

"Come hither, Ash." I steer her toward an upholstered dining chair. At the last second I sit down first, so that she lands in my lap.

"I'm still mad at you," she says as I swing her long legs across my lap and wrap my arms around her.

"Okay." I run a hand down her back until I reach her plaid-covered rump, and I give it a nice, dirty squeeze. "I kinda like the naughty schoolgirl look you're rocking today. The shoes should really be sleazier, though."

"Fuck right off," she says, but her body angles closer to mine, and her breathing accelerates. Her lips brush over the scruff on my jaw. "You're so prickly."

"That's usually my line."

She huffs out a laugh, and her breath on my neck gives me goosebumps. "I mean your *face*. Never saw you with whiskers before."

"It works for you, doesn't it?" The fact that she's noticed lights me right up. My hands are full of Ash, and my cock begins to feel nice and thick beneath her weight.

"Scruff is less pristine. More macho."

"Hmm." I run a hand down her sleek hair. "That's your thing, isn't it? You tell the whole world you want to run the show. But what you really want is for me to throw you up against the wall like a scene from *Outlander*."

Her breath hitches. "You watch *Outlander*?"

"They had it playing at the place where I get my manicures," I lie, just to push her buttons.

She snorts. "Of course they did. Because they weren't expecting any dudes to show up."

"I have a regular Tuesday appointment," I whisper in her ear. I let my lips graze the delicate edge, and she goes absolutely still in my arms. "Can't have rough hands." I pause so I can drop an open-mouthed kiss onto the satiny skin of her neck. "Have to be smooth..." My lips walk a path down her throat, and she shudders. "Smooth hands will feel better on your pretty little clit while I'm making you come."

She whimpers, and I take advantage of it. I turn her perfect chin and lock our gazes. That's when Ash notices how near we are to each other—and how easy it would be for her to lean in and fit our mouths together.

With a soft moan, she does just that. Sweet lips touch mine. Tentatively at first. But the kiss is just as good as it was that time in the pantry, so it's mere seconds later that she tightens her grip on my body. I part her lips with my tongue and wait for her moan.

"*Ohhh.*"

There it is. Ash and I are a much better team than she would care to admit. I stroke her tongue and she shivers, turning in my arms, tossing a knee across my lap to straddle me.

And it's *on*.

Not thirty seconds later we're grinding and groaning. She's riding my lap in imitation of, well, riding my lap. Ash is losing her mind a little. She loves to be on top, because she thinks that's where she belongs. I'd love to press her up against the nearest hard surface and show her how good it could really be, but I can't. She probably has a bump on the back of her head that's my fault.

So I'll have to be content with her bouncing on my dick here in this chair.

I've got my hands running up her legs, pushing up that skirt and she does this little thrust that makes me gasp. In the pantry, we had mouths and tongues on each other, but I wasn't inside her, and all that separates us is a few thin layers of clothing. I groan a little. Can't be helped because Ash....Ash is a fucking goddess.

"I want..." Ash breathes and I am hanging on her next word. Please say she wants me. *Please please please.*

But the universe thwarts me when instead of hearing *"I want you inside me, Braht, you huge man,"* I hear instead...

"Yooooooooo hoo! Is anyone home?"

Ash gasps and practically leaps off of me. She straightens her clothing, pulling down that god-awful yet infinitely fuckable plaid skirt. Even worse, she won't meet my eyes. "Who's there?" she says, a little hitch in her voice that I am very proud of.

The sound of footsteps spurs me to action, by which I mean I adjust my spur and let my polo shirt fall over the tent I'm pitching in my trousers.

A little old woman appears in the doorway of Tom's dining room. "Niiiiice!" she says, then cackles. It's not a creepy cackle. It's more like the cackle old grandmas make at a holiday arts and crafts fair when they've just found the perfect tea cozy. She fingers the collar of her flowered sweatshirt as she admires Bramly's work.

There's something I'd like to finger right now and it's not a sweatshirt.

"Great aesthetic," the woman says. "*Love* the art! That's a man who has the whole package." She giggles again, delighted. "Can I see the rest of the house? I saw the For Sale sign in the yard, and the front door was open..."

"Of course!" Ash says with too much cheer, although this woman is obviously just a nosy neighbor, not a potential buyer. She's wearing her freaking slippers.

But my Ash snaps right into realtor mode. "I'm Ash Power. It's so nice to meet you. Here is my card. You'll notice that I'm a waterfront home specialist." Her spine straightens as she taps the card and hands it over. She smiles widely, the way an electric eel might smile before snatching down its prey.

I wish I were the prey.

Not a glance for me, though. This interruption is working just fine for her.

Ah, well. We'll connect eventually. You can't hold back what's meant to be. I totally believe that. All the self-help audiobooks I've been listening to confirm it.

The old lady is in the kitchen already, exclaiming over the top-notch appliances. I hear Ash say, "Thirty thousand BTUs!" My honey is selling the heck out of the Wolf range, possibly in order to make her escape from me.

I can't resist. I must enter the fray.

My erection enters it first, preceeding me into the kitchen. "Have you seen the butler's pantry?" I crow. "Ash and I have a thing for pantries. It's right over here."

"Oooh!" the old lady says, following me like a happy puppy. Does she give my tent an appreciative glance? Does she? I'd like to think so.

"And then we'll see the boathouse," I offer. "You don't want to miss the boathouse. A rather famous sex tape was shot there. Right this way."

Ash gives me a growl, just as I knew she would.

I'll be thinking about that growl later tonight when I...um...take matters into my own hands. Literally.

Then I'll watch the next episode of *Outlander*. I've got to learn to channel me some Jamie Fraser.

5 FALL FESTIVAL FIASCO

Ash

"How do you like my balls?" Brynn asks me.

She's referring to a new recipe for deep-fried blue cheese nuggets. I swear they cause spontaneous orgasms whenever I pop one into my mouth. Then again, that's pretty much what happens *whenever* I pop any kind of ball in my mouth.

It's, uhm, been a while.

"They're scrumptious," I say, referring to the balls. The cheese fritters. *Sigh*. My mind is elsewhere, and it's completely the fault of one overdressed coworker.

Today Brynn and I are sharing a booth at the Fall Festival Fandango. There are a lot of F's in that name, but it's basically all the great things about fall wrapped up in a Saturday afternoon. Crisp weather. Excellent food. And business opportunities. Brynn is promoting her blog and books, and I'm promoting, well, me. I have a fresh stack of business cards to scatter like seeds in the wind. I should be all fired up to find new clients.

And yet I'm not. It's strange.

My bestie gives me a hip bump. "What is wrong with you? It's a beautiful day, and I've fed you four different ball-shaped foods.

Sadie is off buying us apple pie, pumpkin fritters and coffee. That's like, all the best things in life, except bacon. Why so glum?"

"I'm not glum," I grumble. But she's right. I'm glum on a *perfect* day. We're at a fall festival in an apple orchard that's heavy with fruit. Behind us is a corn maze and off in the distance, a horizon of trees in reds, oranges and yellows. Booths line the orchard, tucked in between the trees. We're well fed, and I'm wearing cashmere, because fall. Also, because cashmere is just plain sexy and decadent. What could be better than this?

"Rough week?" she pries. "Are you ever going to tell me how that VanHeimlich showing went?"

I let out a little moan of despair, but then I swallow it down because I need to appear friendly. I look around at all the happy families and couples. Everyone here is wearing scarves and looks like they stepped off the set of *Gilmore Girls*. Brynn has a cute banner advertising her food blog Brynn's Balls and I'm handing out luggage tags with the VanderMollen Real Estate logo on them, along with my phone number. Always be prepared for luck.

Only my heart isn't really in it. I'm too busy kicking myself over that fiasco with Braht. I fell for his fucking antics. *Again*. And then I disgraced myself by rubbing him as thoroughly as if I were trying to wax his Beemer with my body. That guy is my kryptonite. Even worse—his desk is now six feet away from me at work. Everywhere I turn, he's there!

I'd be creeped out by it if I wasn't secretly turned on.

"Hey, is that your phone?" Brynn asks just as Steve Miller's "Take The Money and Run" starts playing from my pocket. "Whose ringtone is that?"

I yank out the phone and look at the digits. "It's my ring for an unidentified local number." I'm a realtor, so I answer in a hot second. You never know when the next big client is going to show up and change your life. Or at least pay you a fat commission. "Hello, this is Ash Power of VanderMollen Realty's Eastown branch! How may I help you?"

The caller doesn't say anything, though. I press the phone against my ear and wait, expecting to hear at least a robocall start up. All I hear is someone's sigh. It feels familiar somehow.

The hair stands up on the back of my neck. "Hello?" I say again. "Is there anyone there?"

I hear a click. And then nothing.

That's weird. Weird, but hang-ups happen, right? Especially those robocalls. It was probably some poor salesperson calling to tell me how I've won a vacation and all I'll have to do is give them my credit card and my first-born child. Yep. That's what it was.

Okay.

Good.

It was definitely not my ex-husband stalking me from prison. This is where my mind goes in October, I guess. Because it's almost Halloween, so a hang-up would make anyone feel like she's starring in somebody's horror film.

It would, right?

"You also didn't tell me how it went with Zelda," Brynn prods.

"Zelda isn't real," I remind her.

"No kidding. But what did Braht say when there was no assistant Zelda?"

I squint up at the perfect sky. "He didn't even mention her. Probably because I wasn't very convincing." Having Braht in the office these past two days hasn't been easy. "I wish he'd just go back to the branch across town and leave me alone."

Brynn gives me a sideways glance. "Too distracting?"

Definitely. But that wasn't even the biggest problem. "You know I win the branch sales bonus every year, right? I'm worried that now I won't get the prize. And I've already spent it."

"Oh, honey. On what?"

"Home repairs. I put a down-payment on a new garage door." Also a top-notch home security system, but that's just me being paranoid, so I don't mention it. "Braht's numbers from the other branch shouldn't count, right?" I hope management will realize that's unfair.

I'm really not good at sharing. Or compromising. I know this.

Luckily I am saved from further self-flagellation when a cute family approaches our table. The school-aged boys help themselves to one of Brynn's apple cinnamon balls. The mother takes one of Brynn's measuring spoons, with *Brynn's Dips and Balls* printed on the handle.

"Would you like a luggage tag?" I offer a black one to the dad —the macho color.

"I'd love one." He reads the back. "VanderMollen, huh? We might be needing to upsize." He reaches over to pat his wife's belly, and I notice she's pregnant.

"Oh!" I say, feeling suddenly better. I live for these moments. "If you'd like me to run you a report of available four-bedrooms in your neighborhood, I'm happy to do it."

"That might come in handy," he agrees.

I slide exactly the right business card out of my pile. This one says, *Ash Power, Family Expansion Specialist*. I have a total of ten different business cards, each one proclaiming me a specialist at something slightly different.

A girl has to put her best self forward at all times. God knows the men of the world have always done so.

"Thanks!" The guy pockets my card, and the family moves off toward one of the food tents.

But now that they're gone, my burst of enthusiasm goes, too. It smells like a pumpkin spiced latte threw up around here. I am definitely not feeling at peace with the fall spirit. I want to sneer at the decorative corn and smash all the pumpkins. I don't know what this rage is exactly.

Sadie strolls up with her twin girls in tow. They're more than a year old now, and they're pretty fucking cute. They walk in a teetering way, as if every step is a fifty-fifty chance of a face-plant. "We brought coffee!" Sadie says. God, I hope the twins aren't carrying it. I sigh with relief when I see Sadie has a gigantic thermos tucked into her stroller.

She's got everything in that stroller. Granola bars, diapers, juice, Neosporin. I sorta want to ask if her husband is in that stroller, tucked away somewhere, but I refrain. Something is going on with them, yet I still have hope for her. Maybe everything will turn out fine. Maybe her husband will prove us all wrong and turn out to be a decent guy. Doubtful, though.

But back to the coffee. I reach for the thermos, tempted to take a swig. "You are the best!" I exclaim with a whole lot of vigor. It's possible that I'm under-caffeinated. I pour some of the liquid gold into a tiny paper cup and slug it back. With a quick swipe of my mouth, I'm almost good to go. In fact, I'm starting to feel generous. It must be the caffeine.

"Ladies," I offer to the miniature people. "Want a luggage tag? I have pink ones!"

The twins pounce, but they reach for the black ones. Oh! Power color. I make a mental note of deep respect again.

Actually, I am very glad they're pouncing at the luggage tags and not my ankles. I'm just not one hundred percent pro-children. They're just so...grabby.

And then I'm suddenly side-tracked when a male voice asks, "Got one of those in titanium?"

My nipples harden instantly. Damn it! That can only mean one thing. "Braht," I say, raising my chin. "What are you doing here?"

The crowd parts before him, and, God, he's like a walking ad for *GQ*. He's got on a long, fitted camel coat, russet-colored pants, and he's wearing loafers. Actual fucking loafers. All he needs is an ascot to complete the picture. I shake my head and try to focus.

"I am here with amazing news!" he says and smiles that shit-eating cocky grin that has surely brought many women to their knees for him. Including me, damn it.

I dig my heeled boots into the dirt. There will be no kneeling for me. "What's your news?" I demand, crossing my arms over my chest. It's a body stance that sends the signal of dominance.

Also, it covers my tight, hard nipples.

"Come here," he says.

"No."

"Come here and I'll tell you."

"Not happening."

Brynn is watching us and moving her head like it's a tennis match. "For fuck's sake!" she says and then pushes me and I stumble, right into Braht's outstretched, soft arms. What the fuck is this coat made of? I want to rub my face up and down it. I swear to God I feel his arm muscles flex beneath my fingertips. And goddammit. Why's he have to smell so good, and clean...and fresh.

He holds me to him for a second and leans by my ear. There's a puff of breath against my skin and all the hairs on my arm rise, and then he breathes "We. Sold. The. House. For cash."

WHAT THE FUCK?

"What the fuck?" I ask aloud. "To whom? At what price?" My business brain does a little catalogue of all the possibilities, and then I can't help the grin that blooms on my face. "Wait! The little old lady in the *slippers*? No way!"

"Yes way. At the asking price, too. Well done, honey bear."

"The one who liked your boudoir photos?" I really can't wrap my head around it.

"That's her! And she's paying cash! She's a famous thriller writer whose book was just made into a film! She even wants to keep the photos!"

It's really too much to take in. That must explain why my brain shorts out and I find myself hugging Braht a moment later. Suddenly we're jumping up and down and giggling. And it goes on and on. With more hugging.

"Ash!" I hear Brynn say, but I can't stop myself. It's fall and I'm surrounded by chrysanthemums and the world is *good* and Braht and I just made a shitload of money on a cash sale! "Oh God, Braht!" I exclaim. This is better than coffee. Or even bacon. The adorable fucking orchard cannot even contain my joy!

Then his hand is on my lower back and he's pulled me up against his hard chest. And I see it happen in slow motion. His beautiful mouth swoops in and locks against mine. The kiss is pure sizzle. I fuse myself to Braht without stopping to think why I'd do such a thing. Again! But Braht can fucking kiss. Like, ahhhhhhhh. My brain takes a short nap, but my ovaries stand up and whistle.

"Ash..." I hear Brynn's voice somewhere in the distance. I'm too busy to pay attention because kissing Braht feels fucking amazing until she says my name again, this time with an edge of panic in her voice.

I push against Braht and he pulls away. It takes a minute for my eyes to focus, and when they do, Braht and I are staring at each other, panting like we've just run a sprint.

"Ash!"

I finally turn, and it's immediately clear what Brynn was trying to warn me about.

"Oh!!! Hunter!" my mother squeals. "It's *soooo* good to finally meet you! This is great!"

She and my father rush both of us. A split second later their handmade-sweater-encased arms surround me and Braht until we're a big old sandwich of family love.

Holy. Shit.

"Tell me you're coming to Thanksgiving!" my mom squeals.

And then Braht...the fucker...he wrecks it. He says: "Of course! Wouldn't miss it for the world!"

Noooooooo!

Suddenly my father grins and my mother starts babbling. "This is amazing! Finally! Oh my goodness! This is going to sound ridiculous," she says with another giggle. "But I was starting to think you were a figment of Ash's imagination!"

Brynn claps a hand over her mouth so she won't burst out laughing. I don't see what's so damned funny. I fight off my parents and literally collapse into a heap on the grass.

Goddamn Braht.

6 TURKEY, PIE, AND SOME KIND OF BLUE

Braht

Keeping my hands at ten and two on the steering wheel, I glance at Ash. She's sitting ramrod straight in the passenger seat of my BMW, looking like she'd rather commit a cold-blooded murder than have me accompany her to dinner at her family's lake cottage.

We just had a very silent day at work together. She didn't even squawk when I stole one of her carefully sharpened pencils. I almost reached over to check her pulse, but I'm pretty sure it would have resulted in a knee to the groin.

My girl is mad at me for inserting herself into a family holiday. But, seriously, the whole thing is a big misunderstanding. There I was at the fall festival, very innocently making sweet love to her mouth when a loud Mom Voice cries, "Oh, Hunter! We've always wanted to meet you!"

It was trippy.

A good friend always plays along, right? So I accepted Mrs. Power's dinner invitation because it was the polite thing to do. And because Thanksgiving is more than a month away.

Or so I thought.

"You can't be mad forever," I whisper into the silence. The German engineering of my luxury car ensures that we can't even hear any engine noise.

Ash grunts unhappily.

"I didn't *know*, honey bear."

She growls.

"You never told me about your family's weird holiday traditions. I thought it was harmless to accept your mother's Thanksgiving invitation. We could have broken up before the fourth Thursday of November. Saying yes was supposed to be a joke between us kids."

"Our family traditions aren't weird," she bites out. "And if you call me *honey bear* in front of my parents, I will twist off your nuts and serve them to you with gizzard gravy."

"Gizzard gravy. Now that's weird." She gives me a little harrumph at that, so I try again. "Come on, now. You have to admit that it's weird to celebrate Canadian Thanksgiving when you're not Canadian."

This is the source of Ash's current snit—her mother's Thanksgiving invitation wasn't for late November—it was for a mere forty-eight hours after she caught me sucking face with her daughter. I didn't know they celebrated Canadian Thanksgiving. Which is just wrong. For one, it's in October. For two, it's on a Monday.

"Dad is from Toronto," Ash says through her teeth. "I'm half Canadian."

I look over to see if she gives a secret Tim Horton's salute. I make a clicking noise that's meant to indicate doubt and also to remind Ash that I have a tongue. A tongue she really enjoyed in a certain pantry. "Aren't Canadians famous for being nice, though?"

My next sound is something like *oof* because she's reached across the steering column to punch me in the kidney.

"I'm sorry," she says quickly. "Physical violence is uncalled for. This is all just so awkward."

Since I'm not a stupid man, I don't point out that Ash should never have pretended to have a boyfriend named Hunter in the first place. I wouldn't be driving to her parents' lakefront cottage right now if it weren't for her original deception.

"It doesn't have to be so awkward," I say gently. "What if we didn't pretend? For twenty-four hours, I'm your guy."

"W...what? That makes no sense."

Ah, well. It was worth a try. "It makes just as much sense as your plan," I argue.

"I don't have a plan."

"Exactly."

She pouts.

"Is it really so insane? Would you never date a guy like me?"

"We work together."

"Pfft." *Nice try, Ash.* "That's not the problem and you know it."

"Okay, fine. The real problem is that real men don't say *pfft*. Or wear Ferragamo loafers. Or cry during dog food commercials."

"There was something in my eye." There was, too. Maybe. But the puppy was really cute, and when the family brought him home from the pound, it just spoke to me. "None of that, by the way, is the reason you're so scared of me."

"I am *not* scared of you," Ash says quickly.

I cough into my hand. "*Bullshit.* Not me specifically. You are afraid of letting go. Terrified."

The speed at which she turns to face the window is confirmation of the problem. I can read her like a glossy magazine.

"Letting go can be fun," I remind her. "I'll show you later, when you strip off my Lacoste and Ferragamo with your teeth."

"I don't like you very much," she says in a small voice.

"You'll like me better when I've tied you to the bed in your parents' cottage."

She makes a noise that's half rage, half lust. Oh, I've got her number. I really do.

"I brought four neckties in preparation. Hermès, of course. Very silky."

"You're delusional."

Maybe. But the conversation is brought to a halt by a female voice saying, "*Dans deux kilomètres, prenez la sortie quinze pour Bear Lake.*"

"Oui, madame!" I reply. "Merci beaucoup!"

"Of course your GPS is set to speak French," Ash mumbles. "Of course it is."

"It's great practice," I point out. "*Hunter* has to impress your parents. How's your French, Ash?"

"Je déteste tes entrailles," she says. *I hate your guts.*

"Okay, pretty decent, then."

She actually turns to give me a wry smile. "You're a good sport, Braht. Have I ever told you that?"

"No. You usually leave that part out."

"I'm sorry," she whispers. "My parents make me a little crazy. They're a little overprotective. It makes me jumpy. I'll try to tone down the bitch mode, if you try not to embarrass me. Too much."

"Oui, madame." I take the next exit. We're almost there. I can hear the waves crashing in the distance.

"Turn here," Ash says.

"Where?" I ask. The GPS is curiously silent.

"At the fish! THE FISH!"

What fish? Oh! *That* fish. It's a battered windsock. I wrench the wheel and turn onto a tiny little gravel road that just climbs up and up. And up. I didn't know roads could be built at a 90 degree angle. But my German luxury car is well-engineered. We've done worse together.

"You have to gun it at the top," Ash says. I look over at her and she licks her lips. Those lips that were once perfectly around my cock. Suddenly Ash reaches over and runs her hand down my leg. If she moves it up a little bit she's going to get a surprise. A big, hard surprise. "Gun it!" she yells, pressing down on my knee to force my foot down on the accelerator.

The car lurches uphill. "Towanda!" I scream. Is that a

reference to *Fried Green Tomatoes?* Why, yes it is. It was on HBO and has aged really well.

In a show of solidarity, Ash screams with me.

If only I could get her to scream *my* name.

Ash

I thought Braht was going to have a heart attack, but he survived the ascent to my parents' cottage. The house is tucked into the woods. First you go up this super-steep hill, then wind your way down to the beachfront. And there sits our place. It reminds me of Brynn and Tom's new place, but their cottage is more architectural beautiful, whereas this cottage is more it's-been-in-my-family-for-75-years-and-it-still-stands.

The house is small, with chocolate-brown shingles and a stone front. There's a screened-in porch overlooking the beach below. The doors are short so—unless you're a hobbit—you have to duck to enter. And the floors are all slanted because the house is built on a dune. You can't even get permits to build here anymore, so we just deal with the unevenness. We've all learned to lean. And the furniture has been adjusted so that it's all lopsided. Or rather it would be if we ever tried to reuse these chairs somewhere else.

Which we never will, because this is the Power Place. It's our family sanctuary. It's where I go to escape for a while, where I can be a kid again and my mom brushes my hair while Dad makes hot chocolate from scratch.

I love my parents, but they often make me crazy. Ever since my life blew up five years ago, they've become the most overprotective people in the world. They mean well, but it's a little hard to take. I can't even explain this to poor Braht, who's getting all their laser-like attention, because I do not talk about Dwight. Not ever. Not with anyone. If I don't talk about him, then he's not real and not a threat.

My parents show Braht to the upstairs bedroom. "We put you two up here, where there's some privacy," my mother says. I pretty much want to die, because that means she's imagining that I have sex with Braht.

Since I imagine that pretty often, too, I guess that makes two of us.

My dad ushers us outside for a pre-dinner moment on the porch. The last of the day's slanting sunbeams warm us while jazz filters out to from the living room. Miles Davis. "Some Kind Of Blue."

It's Dad's favorite. He likes to listen to Miles while he cooks. Mom is not a cook—she's the type to produce takeout meals and dessert. She can make exactly one killer dessert, and I look forward to having some later.

For now, I can hear the waves on the shore, while the scent of roasting turkey curls around us. The air is cool and beautiful, and everything is right with the world.

Mom hands out portions of hot cider, and I wrap both my hands around the mug, reminding myself to stay calm. Braht is sitting next to me looking all smug and infinitely fuckable. And Mom sits in a rocker, watching Braht and me with undisguised curiosity.

I have to hand it to Braht. He's played his role perfectly so far. He charmed the pants off my parents when we arrived. He carried both our bags into the house and made all the right noises of admiration during the nickel tour.

Now he's right beside me on the porch swing, one leg crossed primly over the other, one of his arms draped casually over my shoulder. He's laughing at a dreadful joke my father told. Something about a chipmunk who walked into a bar.

I'm clutching my mug in both hands, trying not to notice his clean, expensive scent.

Or the fact that my nipples are hard.

A timer dings from inside the kitchen. "I'll get it!" my mom says.

I use it as an excuse to leap to my feet. "Can I help?" I follow my mother inside, leaving Braht to fend for himself with Dad.

Mom and I set the table together. "It's so nice to finally meet your man," my mother says. She is *giddy*.

Naturally I feel like the worst daughter on Earth. Not only am I deceiving her, but making Braht play along, too. I can't even think of a suitable response that isn't digging my own grave a little deeper.

I fucking hate deception. I, of all people, should know better.

"He's so...*refined*," my mother continues. "A true gentleman."

The image of Braht stroking his erection on a chaise lounge flits through my brain, and I have to wonder what Mom would say if she knew the real Braht. Heck. She'd probably love him anyway. My mom is on my side no matter what. I should be grateful, but it's often just so stifling.

"Do you think it's...serious?" she asks, hope shining in her eyes.

Oh, hell. "Uh." I try to remember exactly when I invented him. "Too soon, Mom. You have to wait at least eighteen months to ask me that."

She nods and I can almost see her filing away the date as a reference. "Stuart!" Mom calls. "The turkey's brown and has popped a boner!"

She means the turkey timer. She looks at me and raises her eyebrows, and I'm sure she's going to suggest someone else pop a boner and give her some grandchildren already.

To save myself, I volunteer to mash the potatoes, because a girl can't be expected to answer prying questions over the sound of the mixer.

The meal is both lovely and terrifying.

I began the hour worrying that Braht and I hadn't really prepped for this and that the whole charade would come immediately unglued if Braht decided to ad lib in the wrong direction. If he told my parents, say, that he and I were going to hike through the Grand Canyon together, the gig would be up. Because I'd never hike through the Grand Canyon, not unless a sherpa followed me around with a portable shower and a featherbed.

My parents have known me for thirty-five years, right? Their bullshit meter is well calibrated.

Or is it? Everything Braht says at the table makes my mother smile. *Everything*. She wears the expression of a lovesick puppy all throughout the meal. She fawns over him, offering each dish three times. At least.

It's going pretty well when I almost wreck it without his help. "Braht, can you pass the butter?" I ask. And the second the words leave my mouth, I hear the error.

"Braht?" my mother asks.

"Nickname!" I squeak.

Braht shrugs calmly. "Fraternity brothers. They thought Hunter was a stuffy surname."

"What's your first name, then?" my father asks. "Ash always refers to you as Hunter."

"Ah. My first name is Sebastian."

Sebastian. It suits him. It really does. Not that I care.

Let's face it, Braht is a little too good at slipping into the boyfriend role. He dons it like a cardigan sweater. He has an answer for every one of my parents' questions. He calls us an "office romance" even though all I've done is glare at him since he appeared in my branch of the realty for the first time last week.

Then my mother asks how we became a couple, and I have a moment of pure terror wondering what he'll say. And since I've just put a roasted Brussels sprout in my mouth, I can't even leap into the breach and take charge of the question.

I'm still chewing as Braht tells my mother that he noticed me the very day I went into the downtown location for my job interview. He tells her that he hid behind stacked cartons of copy paper to get a better look at me sitting in the owner's office.

I can't help being impressed at the way he makes the whole thing sound believable. And oh, the irony. My real job interview happened at the lowest point in my life, just a few months after I'd lost my former job in a commercial real estate firm. It's easy to get fired when your husband has been indicted for embezzling money from your employer.

After I finally extricated myself from Dwight's criminal activities—by proving to the police that I wasn't a criminal, only the world's biggest idiot—I'd begged every real estate firm in West Michigan for a job. It was only by luck that VanderMollen gave me a second chance. They were opening a new branch and were short of help.

Braht nudges me under the table with his foot. For a second I'm annoyed that he'd try to play footsie, but then I realize I'm spacing out and he's trying to point out that Mom has just asked me a question.

"Sorry?" I flail.

"Ice cream on your pie, honey?"

"Of course," I say quickly.

"I've never known Ash to turn down ice cream," Braht says. He's laying it on pretty thick. But my mother is eating it up with a spoon, and I don't even blame her. Braht is a charming fucker. And so confident. He's practically reclining in his dining chair, wineglass draped in his hand, head thrown back like a wanton lord at the feast. His skin is honey toned in the candlelight.

You know that game—kiss, marry or kill? It's been well documented that I can't decide between kissing Braht or killing him. But after tonight, I think my mother will assume we're halfway to the altar.

This is bad. She's going to be devastated when we break up.

Dessert is mom's Dutch apple pie and coffee. I try to eat it slowly, because this is my favorite dessert in the world.

"Eat up, Ashley," my dad says, frowning at me. "You're a little thin. Been workin' too many hours again?"

"No," I argue immediately. Even if it's true. The month of October always stresses me out. It's the anniversary of Dwight's imprisonment.

"We know you always feel a little tense in the fall," my mother says softly.

Goddamn parents. They're going to ruin this moment, when I'm supposed to be communing with a slice of pie. I search my brain for a change of topic and come up blank.

"Did Ashley tell you I'm taking her to a spa next week?" Braht asks.

"What? That sounds lovely." My mother beams at him.

"True story," Braht says, even though it's an utter lie. "Nothing but good food and massages for three days straight. Mani-pedi beside the pool. The works."

My father gives Braht an appreciative glance, and my mother forgets to prod me. She offers everyone another scoop of ice cream instead.

And for a moment I forget that this is just a big scam. I admire Braht's fine features in the candlelight and wonder how it would feel to have side-by-side pedicures beside a pool.

Then I give myself a mental slap and finish my pie.

7 THE TOWER OF POWER

Braht

Dinner is a blast. I eat my weight in turkey with all the fixings, while Ash watches nervously. The Power family indulges in all the usual Thanksgiving foods, except there's also green tomato chow served with a slice of tourtiere, a spiced meat pie.

Usually they have tourtiere for Christmas, Marie, Ash's mom, tells me, but she remembered Ash mentioning something about Hunter loving meat.

It's really startling how much Ash's fake boyfriend and I have in common. It's almost like Ash was describing me. Now, it's true I wax vegetarian at times, but that's just to cleanse the old Brahtty system. I do, on occasion, appreciate a good piece of meat. I appreciate it even more when Ash appreciates my meat. *Ahem.* Anyway. Those pies! They're so good I want to roll around in the leftovers.

Canadian Thanksgiving. Who knew?

After dinner I wash dishes with Mr. Power, and we compare all our favorite golf courses. I can't help but like her parents and be a little envious of Ash. This is what a healthy, normal family looks like. A warm house, soft lighting, great food, and they're actually here. So unlike my own family.

Talking to Ash's parents is easy. Talking to Ash...is less easy. If only she'd give in to the inevitability of us.

"I like your folks," I say an hour later as I lie in bed.

"Braughsntt. Rawrrkakt," she says from the bathroom. She's brushing her teeth.

"When you and I are married, your parents and I will get along great."

I hear a choking sound from the bathroom. Then violent spitting, followed by rinsing. "I'm not even going to dignify that with a response," she says eventually.

Grinning up at the ceiling, I realize I'm having more fun than I've had in a long time. It's not my fault if Ash is stressed out from a long evening of deception. Lord knows I've had plenty of practice imagining what life would be like if we were a couple. I played my role perfectly. It wasn't even hard.

Other things are hard, though. And when Ash walks out of the bathroom a minute later, she actually gasps. "Jesus Christ."

The sheet is covering my erection. Sort of. I'm as hard as my Big Bertha driver, and my cock is pointing at the ceiling. It's not my fault, though. I'm well fed, and Ash is wearing a threadbare Pink Floyd T-shirt that might be a relic from the eighties. When she moves, her breasts press against the soft fabric of the moon and jiggle a bit.

It's that press and jiggle that gets me.

Slowly I wrap my hand around the base of my cock, pulling the sheet tight, giving her an even better view. "You've seen it before," I point out. "But I'm happy to give you another look..." I stroke myself again. It feels good, stroking myself, her watching me. I think I see her nipples starting to pebble.

"Why are you naked under there?" Her face flames.

Dumbest question ever. "I'm still in character, honey bear. And Hunter wants you. Badly. But I don't think you're playing your role very well right now."

Actually she is, though. Her eyes are dilated. And her gaze can't decide where it wants to land. She takes in my bare chest and my arm muscles flexing as I stroke myself over the sheet. Then she focuses in on the Tower of Power itself.

"Have another taste?" I invite her. It's a miracle that I can say this casually, because I'm dying right now. That hungry look on her face is everything. "You did such a great job last time. Most women can't handle me."

She swallows roughly and closes her eyes. "You have the biggest ego I ever saw."

"You can't see my ego, sweetie. You can only see my cock. My fraternity brothers referred to it as The Bratwurst."

"Wait." Her eyes pop open. "You changed your last name after college. To Braht."

"Yeah." *Stroke. Stroke.* Unnngh. I'm watching her lips move and wishing they were worshipping my dick.

"Oh my god." She puts her hands on her hips. "Some men name their dicks. But you named yourself after your dick?"

"Don't judge. It's a little inside joke I have with myself." Reluctantly I take my hand off the Bratwurst and tuck my arms behind my head. My Tower of Power stands firm. "Kill the light, baby."

"I'm not your baby." She grabs the other pillow off the bed. "I'm sleeping on the floor."

"No you're not." I grab the pillow back from her.

"Then *you're* sleeping on the floor."

"Also not happening."

She glares.

I smile. "Ashley, I'm not going to touch you."

"You're not?" Is that disappointment on her face? Of course it is.

"Nope." I pat the bed. "Get in. Believe me—I'm not a fan of fucking women who aren't begging for it. We'll just talk."

Her mouth opens and then closes again. She turns out the

light, and I feel her slip into bed beside me. "Men don't talk," she says.

"This one does. I'm not like other men, Ash. I'm Man 2.0."

There's a pause, then she says "Thank you for coming."

"Unng." Nobody is coming. Not the way I need to.

"I...I don't know why I feel the need to lie to my parents. They've been worried about me. I'm an only child, and they can be pretty intense."

"They're awesome, Ash. They obviously love you." My own parents kicked Bramly and me to the curb more than a decade ago, leaving me to fend for myself and raise their younger kid. Good times.

"I know. I'm trying to apologize. Inventing Hunter was a cheap thing to do, and I learned my lesson." She rolls over onto her belly, her cheek on the pillow. My eyes have adjusted to the moonlight, so I can see the perfect curve of her cheek as she gazes at me. "Really, I've been a terrible grouch."

"I forgive you." *I'll do anything for you, silly girl.*

"Now what did you want to talk about?" She blinks in the dim light.

"Oh, nothing big. I just wanted you to know how much I enjoyed dinner."

"Thank you. Really. I'm glad."

"Everything was so tasty. I mean—don't get me wrong, there are even tastier things in the world."

"Such as?"

"Your thighs. Your skin is so sweet, honey bear." She really does smell like honey. It drives me wild. "My tongue *loves* that spot where your leg meets your pussy."

"Braht!" she gasps.

"I know. The truth is sometimes hard to hear. But I'm being honest here. I want to lick you all over. I wonder if you'd taste different in the bed than in the pantry? We could find out. You could lie right there and spread your legs. Maybe fuck yourself against the mattress while I put my tongue in your pussy."

"Stop," she pants, even though I can feel her hips shifting on the bed. "Even if we were a c-couple we wouldn't do it in my parents' house." She whispers the last part.

"Sure we would. When we're a couple, you'll be the most sexually satisfied woman in Michigan. If this bed creaks, I'll just take you into the shower and fuck you up against the tiles."

"Knock it off, Braht," Ash says. But then she gives an honest-to-god shiver of desire.

Fuck. A new wave of wanting rocks through me. "You'll be happy to know that this fun little chat is torturing both of us."

She puts her face in the pillow and laughs.

"We can play this a couple of different ways. You can come over here and climb on my dick and ride me like a cowgirl who's heard the dinner bell on fried chicken night. Or we can both roll over, facing opposite directions, and stare off into the deep abyss of loneliness."

"Overdramatic much?" she asks. Then she gives a little moan into the pillow. "Gaaaahh. I love fried chicken. And sex. Stop talking now."

"Fine. But I'm not going to touch you unless you ask me to."

There is silence on Ash's side of the bed. She's thinking hard over there. All I can hear is the pounding of the waves against the beach outside.

"Just so you know," I add. "...I put a condom on the night table next to me, just in case. Size XL." I wait. Anything could happen. Everything should.

That's when I hear it. A whimper. Soft. An exhale. She's so turned on she can't hold still. Her hips shift against the bed. "I hate you," she whispers eventually.

"I know, baby duck. I know." I listen to her tortured breathing for another moment before I speak again. "So what are you going to do about it? Feel free to torture me back. Put your hand in your panties. My Ash likes to be in charge, right? Make yourself come, honey. And make me listen to it."

There's just enough light that I can see her eyes narrow. "You'd like that too much."

"Like it and hate it," I admit. "I ache for you already." That is far more honesty than is really wise.

But fuck it. Nothing ventured, nothing banged.

Ash rolls over suddenly. For a long moment nothing else happens. Her expression is unreadable. I actually feel a frisson of nervousness. That's unexpected. I'm not used to feeling tense about anything.

Casually, Ash slides a hand down the bed. She lifts her T-shirt, exposing her boob. Then she cups the swell of her perfect breast, closes her eyes and sighs.

Holy. Fuck. My mouth goes dry, and I watch helplessly while she rolls her nipple. She swallows, and her throat ripples.

And, Jesus. Now I know what people mean when they say, *be careful what you wish for*. This isn't exactly what I'd pictured. I thought I could talk Ash onto my side of the bed.

I've underestimated her. Now she's shucking off that old T-shirt and taking both breasts in her hands. Her back is arched as she plays with her tits.

And I'm dead. Dead!

"Oh," she whispers. "Yessss..."

Kill me already. It's not just that I'm as hard as concrete and my balls are throbbing. Physical discomfort isn't my real problem right now. It's the look on her face and the fact that she's only two feet away. And I'm not allowed to touch.

Every muscle in my body is locked up tight, and I have the urge to sob. Ash has beaten me at my own game.

With one long, sleek leg, she kicks the sheet away and then reaches down to flick her panties off her body.

I'm in agony as she puts a hand between her legs and strokes slowly. Just once.

My chest heaves, and I barely prevent a sound from escaping

my lips. It's a close call, because whatever that sound was, it wouldn't be very manly. I close my eyes for a second and take a deep, calming breath. I call upon my inner resources. My super power is staying cool in a crisis, right?

When I open my eyes again, Ash's fingers are moving in a sweet little circle. My cock twitches, but I've mastered him again. So I'm able to speak in a mostly normal voice when I ask, "Are you very wet?"

She nods, her eyes closed in concentration.

I reach over to the bedside table and take the condom. I tear it open.

Ash's eyes pop open. "What are you doing?"

"Nothing, honey bear. Just imagining how you'd feel bouncing on my dick."

She lets out a shuddery breath, her hand stilling between her legs. "You wish."

"I do." I put the condom on the tip of my cock and slowly roll it down. I'm super-sized right now. The condom barely fits.

Her gaze follows my hand, as I knew it would.

"You only had one piece of pie tonight," I say, taking my sheathed cock in hand.

"W-what?" she breathes.

"Pie. You had one small piece. Not two? Why not?"

She blinks at me helplessly. "Didn't need two."

"I saw you eyeing it," I say, stroking myself. I roll my hips a little, leaning into the pleasure. Two can play at this game. "But you didn't partake. Is that because you didn't want the second piece? Or because you didn't want to be the girl who eats two pieces of pie?"

"Get out. Of my brain," Ash says. "Maybe I wasn't hungry."

"Like you're not hungry for it right now?"

She whimpers. We are no longer talking about pie.

"I don't believe in guilty pleasures, Ash." My voice is a rasp. I stretch on the bed, tucking my hands behind my head again. "Pleasure shouldn't make you feel guilty. There's nobody here but us. Think of how good you could feel over here on this side of the bed."

Her body goes still, and I know she's considering it. I'm playing it cool, but every inch of me wants to have her. I mean, every inch.

She rolls, leans up close to me, whispering in my ear: "I'll tell you what, Braht. Let's make a deal. I like to be in charge. Can you hold still while I do you?"

No way. "Yes, of course."

"You'd better. Just stay right there. Don't move. Don't breathe. Be as silent as you can. If you can do that, I'll join you on your side of the bed."

I blink twice. Because one blink means "yes" and two means "get on my dick before I burst."

Her eyes gleam as she rolls over and silently straddles me. There's more tension in my body than I ever thought possible. I have been wanting this since...forever, and I still don't trust that she'll follow through. I've tasted her, but I've never been inside her.

The bed gives a single, low creak, and I look up into her pretty face and pray.

At dinner tonight I told a story about spying during her first job interview. Ash thinks it was a fabrication, but it was a hundred percent true. Okay, ninety-five percent. It wasn't a stack of copy paper crates that I hid behind. I stood on the other end of the bullpen at the copy machine, sneaking looks at Ash as she spoke to the owner. She turned my crank the very first time I laid eyes on her, with that regal posture and her long neck.

And now she's staring down at me, her silky hair barely covering her nipples, and with a naughty gleam in her eye. "Don't move," she whispers. "I mean it."

"Okay, I..."

She shuts me up with a kiss. Her mouth is hot over mine. And the glide of her tongue is so distracting that I'm already half out of my mind when she begins slowly lowering herself on my length.

Yesssssss!

Without thinking, I push my hips off the bed to take more of her. My punishment is swift and cruel. She lets out a gasp of indignation and pulls off me. "Did you not *hear* me when I said to hold still?"

"Sorry," I murmur.

"No moving." Her eyes flare. I've never met any woman so beautiful in her determination. That spark is why I'm a fish on her line. I fight the hook, but she always reels me in.

"Got it." The words are calm, but my heart is trying to beat its way outside of my body. "Fuck me, honey. Use me up."

Luckily, my dirty talk has encouraged Ash. Her beautiful tits rise and fall as she takes a deep breath, then lowers herself all the way onto my aching cock.

For a moment, once she's taken all of me inside her, we both freeze. My world has teetered on its axis. She's so tight and so gorgeous looking down at me that I can hardly believe we're finally here. And then she moves. *Good god*. I feel every clutching inch of her. I want to reach up and touch her so badly I can't stand it. I bite my lip. Hard.

She moves around, grinding my cock, feeling for the best angle. Or maybe she's just torturing me. If so, it's working. I actually see the moment when she finds what she's looking for. She takes a shuddery breath and bites her lip. Her hips swing in a slow circle while I die of blue balls.

Totally worth it.

"My tits," she whispers, and I take that as permission. I slide my hands up her silky body and cup her breasts, flick the nipples. She moans, and then I just can't hold back anymore. I pull her to me, fusing our mouths while she pistons on top of me. My hands find her delicious ass, and I squeeze her tight.

Suddenly she stops and we freeze again. I'm so busted. She doesn't punish me this time. She gasps instead. I can feel her pussy tighten around my cock as she comes.

The next bit happens in a fever. I quickly roll her over so she's under me. I don't care if I'm making noise. I can't hear the bed creaking because there's a rushing noise in my ears as I claim her, thrusting through her orgasm.

She clenches against me again and again. We are so good together, surely she must feel that with every thrust of my hips. She runs her hands down my back, to my ass, pulling me deeper. The cool breeze off the beach rolls over my sweaty torso. I lean down to kiss her one more time and then my body jerks as I have an orgasm so intense I see stars.

8 AFTERGLOW...GONE

Ash

Goddamn Braht and his fucking amazing bratwurst and sensual skills.

I'm ashamed to admit that after I broke *every one of my own rules* we still don't go to sleep. By three a.m. I've been kneaded and pawed and licked so much I feel like a cat.

I really like feeling like a cat, and I really don't want to feel anything for Braht.

But maybe I don't have to feel. Perhaps this slightly nauseous sensation I have while watching him sleep will pass.

It'd be easy to date him. Picture perfect even.

And *that's* the thing I can't have. Picture perfect isn't real. Nobody's life is a magazine spread. All those beautiful people in real estate brochures aren't real. Those cups of perfectly brewed coffee beside freshly baked croissants are all staged. That's just marketing. Those rooms have been carefully styled and edited to look that way.

You don't see the darkness behind those pictures. You can't see that there was a couple fighting and swearing at each other on that white sofa an hour earlier. And the perfect cup of coffee is really cold and bitter. That croissant has as much flavor as the pages in a book.

I'm lying here beside Braht and free-associating life's miseries because I've seen the chasm that lies between pictures and reality. And that reality is my ex, Dwight.

Cue the shudder I always experience when his beady eyes show up in my thoughts.

Braht doesn't have beady eyes, though, my subconscious whispers. *They're clear and blue.*

Still.

The thing I can't figure out about Braht, though, is, what's he selling? How can he be so charming and *GQ*-beautiful and fucking fantastic in bed? What's he hiding? There has to be something. Nobody's that perfect. I learned the hard way. There are worse things than a broken heart.

Dwight nearly broke *me*.

Braht stirs in bed and moans this deep kind of animal moan. I shake the dark thoughts away for a second and just laugh. Because Braht, naked, asleep, and making that sound, is just funny...and I want the picture perfect for a few minutes more.

"Good morning, Beth and Stuart!" Braht says when we finally go downstairs for brunch the next morning. I look at my mom and dad, horrified one of them is going to say, "Oh, just call us Mom and Dad!" because they would. I can see it in their eyes.

Mom hands me a mug of coffee, already mixed with cream. "You want some coffee?" she asks Braht. I swear, she's avoiding my eyes.

Huh.

"Of course I do!" Braht says in a voice so chipper I want to smack him. "But I'll get it myself. You sit. How do you take yours?"

Mom practically flutters she's so pleased by his manners. "Oh, anything is fine. Just black."

"She likes it with cream," I say and slurp my coffee.

Dad is at the stove making crepes. It's our post-Thanksgiving tradition, which we'll do all over again next month. We love Thanksgiving so much we have it twice. But the intensity with which he's regarding the crepe pan is a little weird.

There's tension in the kitchen. Or is there? Maybe it's my imagination. Maybe my parents heard sex noises last night, and they're embarrassed. When I feel Braht's hand moving up and up my thigh under the table, my body reacts with tingles, but my hand pushes him away.

"Are you two headed home this morning?" Dad asks, his voice cautious.

"Well..." Braht hedges, and I just know he's going to suggest Bloody Marys on the beach or something.

"Yes, we are!" I say. "We've got paperwork to wrap up, and I've got a house to show."

"You do?" Braht asks.

"Yes. I always have a house to show."

He gives me a smug little smile. "Sure you do, honey bear. Let me make a phone call and I'll have two to show later today."

That competitive jerk! Who says things like that? And goddamn it, why are my nipples hard?

I pull my coffee cup closer to my chest and frown while Dad pours another crepe into the sizzling pan, then tilts the pan to spread the batter.

Mom sips her coffee. Then she sneaks a glance at me over the rim of the mug. I see my father look over to catch her eye. And then I realize that Braht has distracted me from something important.

"What is wrong?" I ask, maybe a little more loudly than is necessary. Mom looks at Dad and I just know. Every October we worry about the same thing. Every fucking October.

It usually doesn't actually come to pass. Now I'm afraid that it has.

Dad moves the crepe off the stove, even though it's not done yet. He reaches for an envelope propped up beside the toaster. He hands it over to me and then stands behind Mom, his hand on her shoulder.

Fuck.

The envelope is from the Michigan State Board of Corrections, and it's already open, which is fine with me. I've asked them to do that, because otherwise, I don't think I could survive this moment.

"It's different this time, honey," Mom says.

I don't even have to read it now. I can tell by Mom's tone of voice that it's the worst possible news. Dwight has finally made parole. He's going to be released from the penitentiary, and all I want to do is run. Fast and far, far away.

9 NAUGHTY THINGS OFFICE SUPPLIES DO

Braht

"I don't get it," Tom says, shoveling another forkful of sausage into his mouth.

"Exactly," I agree and take a bite of my own food.

I know Tom is trying to say that he doesn't get what happened at the cottage with the letter and all, but I'm thinking more big picture. I don't get what happened after I finally had the most incredible sex of my life...

Why can't Ash admit that we are perfect together? I mean, I saw stars. Literally. And I swear to god the way her toes curled she must've at least seen a comet. A moon.

Something.

I take another bite of my healthy, low-calorie meal. I'm having an egg white omelet with spinach and tomatoes, not because I really like egg whites, but because Tom thinks healthy food is a sacrilege, and I like to push his buttons.

He gives me a thoughtful stare and then finally says, "She got an envelope from her mother. It had been previously opened..." He's still confused.

"Yup. Her mom hands her a letter. Something official looking. I think I saw a government seal."

Tom chews. There is a bit of ketchup in his beard, but I don't want to interrupt his thoughts to tell him. "And then Ash stopped talking to you?"

"Pretty much. She looked really freaked out. *Scared*." I put down my fork, just picturing her face. I hated that look of fear in her eyes. I want to punch whoever put it there. Right in the throat. Our drive back from the lake cottage was somber. Ash was kind to me, but I knew her mind was elsewhere.

"Let's see," Tom says, scraping his plate. "Maybe it was an audit letter from the IRS? That would be enough to make me pee myself. Taxes are terrifying."

"Good to know." I make a note to avoid Tom on April fifteenth. "But Ash isn't the sort of girl to be fazed by a business letter. She would kick some IRS ass and make it cry."

"I can picture that," Tom says. "I'm a little afraid of her sometimes."

"That's because you don't know what makes her tick." I feel some blood flow toward my Burberry boxer shorts just thinking about making Ash tick. And moan. And scream my name...

Suddenly there's a big fist snapping its fingers in front of my face. "Whoa, there, Brahtty. You're zoning out again."

"You would, too." I let out a sigh of longing.

Tom whistles under his breath. "Holy shit. You've got it bad. Actually, you've always had it bad for this girl. Now you've got it worse."

"It's true. Our night together is seared onto my brain."

Tom snorts. "Your brain, or your bratwurst? Same difference?"

I show him my middle finger and then finish my omelet. It's not just the sex that's made me crazy. It's the disappointment. We were so good together. So blazing hot. I thought it was a turning point.

There was this one moment at about two in the morning. We were making love for the third time. She looked deep into my eyes and whimpered "*Sebastian*" before she came. Just like in all my fantasies. Hardly anyone calls me by my first name. It's always Braht, the name I invented to keep my parents safe. Ugh. What Ash and I had, what we did, was epic.

And now she's barely speaking to me.

"I need to figure out what was in that letter," I say for the tenth time.

"Or, here's another idea." Tom slurps his coffee. "You could just leave the girl alone and wait until she asks for your help."

"Like, do *nothing?*"

Over the rim of his coffee cup he gives me a look that says, *yes, dummy. Butt out.*

I hate this idea. "There's ketchup in your beard," I tell him. I am transfixed by his beard. It's new and he looks like Paul Bunyan.

"Stop staring at it," he says. "I like it. More importantly, *Brynn* likes it." He picks up his napkin to wipe at the glistening fur on his face. "You're hoping I'll call Brynn, quiz her, and find out what Ash is hiding, aren't you?"

Of course I am. "What a great idea! Thank you. I accept."

Slowly, Tom shakes his head. "I'll tell her you're worried. But I'm not going to pry. If she wanted you to know, she would have told you herself."

I hate logic.

"You know," I start. "All you need is a...what do Canadians call it? A toque? You need a hand-knitted hat and you'll look just like you're about to cut down some trees along with your big blue ox." I smile. Got him.

"I'm always ready to cut things down. With. My. BIG. Ox."

There's a pause and then we just both start laughing.

The moment I gallop back into the office, my gaze shoots over to Ash's desk.

Empty.

Damn.

Yesterday she was in and out showing her new listing. And running errands. And meeting with clients. We are neck and neck in this year's competition for the huge end-of-year bonus. It's right there on the whiteboard. So while it makes sense that she's out hustling, I'm also pretty sure that it's an easy way of avoiding me. What I don't understand is why.

Even when I called her honey bear, she didn't glare at me. It's like she's not deigning to give me attention.

I fucking hate it.

So now I wander over to her desk again, looking for signs of life. It's neat as a pin, of course. There are a few listing cards arranged on the desk, and I can tell that she's color coded them. The listings with three bedrooms have orange dots and four bedrooms have green. The pens she uses are arranged in ROYGBIV order (thanks, eighth grade science teacher!) So naturally I pull out the red one to rearrange them. But violating science isn't really enough for me, so I take it a step further.

By the time I'm finished a few minutes later, the red pen and the violet one are 69ing on her desk blotter while the orange and the green pen do it doggy style. They're leaning against her stapler for leverage. It's technically tricky to pull off wall sex between the blue and indigo pens, but with the help of some poster putty, I make it happen.

That leaves only the poor lonely yellow pen. So sad. Poor yellow. I'm thinking hard about how to make a pen masturbate when Ash's line rings.

Because I'm feel frisky, I answer it in a faux British accent. "Hello, chap. You've reached Ash Power's line at Ernst VanderMollen Realty. Can I be of service?"

There's a pause, and I wonder if I'm about to be asked to donate to a worthy cause. But then a gruff male voice demands, "I need to speak to Ash. Put 'er on, please."

"So sorry, mate! She's popped out to the chippy for a bit of a munch."

"What?" He huffs into the phone, and suddenly there's a hurricane in my ear. "Never mind. When'll she be back?"

"Soon!" I lie. "Shall I jot down a message? Do you fancy a showing? Which listing?" My accent has taken on a decidedly more cockney sound every time I open my mouth. But something about this caller rubs me the wrong way, and so I want to keep him talking.

"The condo," he says quickly. "I'm calling about the condo."

"Crikey!" But now my Spidey senses are tingling, because I don't think Ash has a listing for a condo. "Would you mean the one on Fallen Fanny Road?" I don't know where my brain gets these things. Maybe it's the stress talking. Or the egg white omelet.

"I think that's the one. Eh, I can't remember the name of it." He clears his throat. "But I definitely want to see it. Here's my number."

Huh. That's a good dodge. This guy is slick. My Spidey senses are still firing. There's an age-old saying: You can't bullshit a bullshitter. And I'm a bullshitter. Pro level. I don't believe this guy is a client at all, but he already called my bluff.

Hmm.

I jot down his digits and then get rid of him. Whoever he is, he's up to no good, and he's killed all inspiration I had for sexing up Ash's office supplies.

I just miss Ash. I want to see her and make her look at me again like she did on Canadian Thanksgiving at her parents'.

So where the fuck is she?

10 CREAM PUFFS AND CRISES

Ash

After Braht drops me off on Tuesday, I make it two whole days without thinking about him at all. Nope. Not even a little bit.

Okay, that's a total lie. But my intentions are pure.

Our shared office is now problematic, so I vow to avoid thinking about him. Or his lips on my neck. Or his real name on my lips. Nope. I will not look at Braht. I will not look at Braht or imagine him in my bed, all buff and flecked with starlight. I will not imagine lowering myself onto his glorious dick, or ever, ever admit that he has a glorious dick.

And because I can't trust myself to do any of these things, I decide to take my business outside the office today. Again.

The truth is, there's another reason I'm avoiding the office. I'm freaked out about that phone message Braht left me the last time I saw him.

That call was from Dwight. I'm ninety percent sure.

Luckily I can afford a day off. We just finished the paperwork for Tom's house, so my bank account *loves* me. The mystery writer lady is now happily surrounded by pictures of Braht in the buff. She actually put that in the contract—that she got to keep the art in the dining room. ...And now I'm back to thinking about him naked.

Fuck.

In a last-ditch effort for sanity, I text my besties. **Need help. Need a drink. But it's not even 11am.**

Sadie immediately responds with: **I need help, too. There's something I need to tell you both. Does drinking count if we also have brunch together?**

I swear I've seen signs that state "It's not day drinking if it's brunch." So I text, naturally: **BRYNN WE NEED BRUNCH.**

Brynn responds: **I've already got the bacon in the oven. This sounds serious. I'll whip up some cream puffs and mimosas.**

I am out the door as soon as I see the word "bacon."

I hightail it to Brynn's. She and Tom are staying in her newly remodeled Victorian home in Heritage Hill. They're here during the week (mostly) and at their swanky cottage on Lake Michigan on the weekends, or when they're filming one of Brynn's cooking shows. And I'm back to remembering that first show where Braht and I were in the pantry, all over each other with lips and tongues and GET OUT OF MY BRAIN, BRAHT.

It must be all the stress. That letter about Dwight's release, coupled with my, uhm, coupling with Braht, makes me miss a stop sign or three, so I'm doubly surprised when I get to Brynn's and see that Sadie is already here. I'm also surprised she's twin-less. She hardly ever leaves Kate and Amy. Usually they're attached to her boobs. Then again, maybe that was a while ago. I don't understand the teat needs of toddlers.

I pull in behind her and there's another thing that surprises me: Sadie doesn't look right. She's rumpled. She's wearing yoga pants. Sadie never wears stretchy clothing. And she's crying so hard that mascara has made two tracks down her face.

Suddenly I'm not really thinking about myself anymore. I'm worried about Sadie. And I'm betting it was her douchebag husband who did this to her.

Men! I will have his balls in a vise grip by sunset.

Sadie looks at me, stumbles and just says "Alcohol".

I haul her inside.

The house smells like sugar bacon. Brynn opens the door and says, "Holy shit." Then we, admittedly somewhat dramatically, drag Sadie over to the couch and sprawl her out.

"What on earth?" Brynn says while I gasp, "Are the kids okay?"

Sadie just nods and then squeezes her eyes shut tightly. One tear escapes anyway.

I look at Brynn and give her a look that I hope says, "Do something!" and not, "I'm constipated." She nods and I hear her run into the kitchen. I look for something maternal to do, so I awkwardly pat Sadie's shoulder. Don't judge! I don't know what to do in situations like this. I can arm wrestle someone into submission, but comfort them? Unless it involves poking them with a stick, I'm not up for that.

Brynn knows, though. She returns with a beautifully cooked, crisp piece of bacon in her hand that she begins to float under Sadie's nose. I flap my hands to help the scent waft. *Waft, bacon, waft!*

One of Sadie's eyes opens and then she pounces and that bacon is gone. It's a little scary. It's like her mouth is a bear trap or something.

We all breathe deeply. If Sadie went for the bacon then everything will be fine. It's our version of checking if someone has had a stroke.

Sadie hasn't. And neither have I.

The atmosphere is really weird in here and I'm waiting for

Sadie to talk. She looks at me like I should do the talking instead, but now I feel like I'm over-imagining the threat of this letter that's burning in my pocket. I look to Brynn because I want to make a full circle of things. There's silence for a beat or two.

Sadie says: "Mike is having an affair."

I say: "Dwight is out of prison."

Brynn says: "I'm pregnant."

And then we just blink at each other.

"Cream puff?" Brynn asks.

―――――

It takes us a minute to process all the information swirling around us. I mean, how do you respond to that? Boo? Yay? Booyay? So we don't say anything for a minute.

Sadie lifts a hand and Brynn and I haul her to her feet. We schlep to the kitchen where Brynn plates bacon, cream puffs, and pouring mimosas for us. For her, she just has the orange juice. That would have been a sure giveaway if we'd started brunch without hearing her news.

Then we smack and drink and sigh and someone giggles. Maybe even me. I mean life is never dull is it? Then I just can't stand it anymore. "Are you *sure* Mike is having an affair and are you *sure* you're pregnant? I mean, I got certified mail about my woes. Show me some proof, honeys."

Brynn rolls her eyes. "I have six pregnancy tests in the bathroom with all the lines in the world and Tom is at the cottage chopping down a tree because he wants to build a crib from scratch. I didn't bother to tell him we've got plenty of time for that. He just needs to put his hands to work. And we can circle back to all this later, but you two...*talk* already."

"I have proof," Sadie grumbles. "I mean, it's true. And I *will* get proof before I confront him. But I don't even want to talk about it right now. If I'm putting everything into perspective, I'm fine and the girls are fine."

"Where are Kate and Amy, anyway?" I ask.

"With my sister. I told her I needed her and she flew in from Atlanta."

"Oh, right. That's nice." Why don't I have a sister who can fly in from Atlanta? That would be really terrific right about now.

Sadie must sense my fear because she turns to me and grabs my hands and looks me in the eyes. "Are. You. Okay?" she asks, and she means it, even though her own life is coming apart at the seams.

I get a little teary myself and I nod. I squeeze her hands and let go. I love these two women with all of my being, but I can't touch them or be hugged right now because I'd probably spontaneously combust. I just need to take a breath and present the facts.

"Dwight was released last week. And I've gotten two hang-ups on my cell phone. Sometimes I get the sense that someone's watching me, but it usually just turns out to be Braht. I mean, he pops up everywhere."

"You should give Braht a collar with a bell," Brynn says. And now I'm imagining him decked out in leathers, wearing a studded collar and crawling on his hands and knees to me. "Yes, mistress!" the fantasy Braht says. "Hmm. A bell?"

"You know, like a cat." Brynn explains.

Ah. Okay. Naturally my mind went straight to the BDSM scene.

"Seriously though," Sadie says. "If you're getting tingling nerves, pay attention to that. That's coming from your gut. And what science is learning now about gut fauna is that it's so complex that the gut might actually be a second brain."

To which I reply, "Ew." Because *ew*.

"Ignore it at your peril," Sadie says, and there's a little more oomph behind her eyes. She's a natural therapist. She delights in helping people. Someone needs to give her an award and a pair of wings. "So listen to your gut and pull back on the gluten."

"Cream puffs don't have gluten," Brynn says. "They're made of magic."

"Seriously, though, do you think he'll come after you? What could he want?"

"Revenge?" Duh. "I testified against him. And then I got an annulment. He screamed BITCH on his way out of the courtroom."

"He can't get to you. No way," says Brynn all fierce like. "Because we are here to protect you. You can stay here and Tom and I..." Brynn looks a little green and she suddenly takes off and runs to the bathroom. We hear the door slam and immediate retching.

"She really is pregnant," I breathe. It's hard to believe but at the same time perfectly right. It's like my friends are growing up without me.

"I don't want to ever go through that again," Sadie says.

"The retching? Or pregnancy?"

"All of it." She says, again in an unlike-Sadie way. She's usually the perfect Earth Mother and very connected to the universe.

"Are you okay? Are you sure he's cheating?" I try to say the word "cheating" tenderly, but it's such an ugly word that it's hard to make it hurt less.

"I will be okay, once I figure out what to do. Ever since the twins were born, he's not the same. He comments on my sagging breasts and the baby weight I never lost. When I'd nurse the twins, I actually saw him grimace. He told me..." She stops.

"Breathe," I say. "It's okay. You're okay."

Her eyes turn red. "He said at first he was just giving me time to heal and be a mom. And later he said it was hard to...get turned on...by someone who was essentially a...dairy cow."

I'm stunned into silence.

We hear the water running and Sadie quickly says "Don't say anything to Brynn. I'm sure Tom will be different. Some men can't handle being fathers. Some men just want to be *boys*."

Brynn returns looking a little better. When she enters we both say "Congratulations!" and she laughs. "I'm pretty sure pregnancy is going to suck," Brynn says.

She looks to Sadie, who says, "It will be beautiful," and I can't tell if she's lying to reassure Brynn or telling the truth.

"Where were we?" Brynn says. "Oh, that's right. Dwight, the maniac, is out of jail and you're getting calls, and you think he may be coming after you."

"I don't know. I'm probably just imagining things."

"And if you're not? If your gut fauna brain, or whatever Sadie called it, is right?"

I think for a moment. More than anything, I don't want to be alone right now. But Brynn and Sadie both have their hands full. Really full.

If I call my parents and tell them I'm spooked, they'll make me move back in with them. That won't do at all. After my annulment and losing my job, I ended up in my childhood bedroom, right there on the My Little Pony comforter, hating my life. It was a low point I don't wish to revisit.

"I just want to keep moving forward," I announce. "I'm going to be strong."

"You have friends," Brynn says softly. "We're here for you."

"I really appreciate that," I say quickly.

"If you need a night away from it all, come stay with Tom and me," Brynn offers.

"I'll do that," I lie. I don't think I can take the two of them together right now. I'm happy that Brynn has found a man who loves her so much he gives her beard rash every time he walks into the room. With her pregnant, they must be unstoppable right now. Like a 24/7 sexfest.

Sadie pats my arm. "I'm here for you, too."

Of course she is—in between negotiating the probable end of her marriage and raising two toddlers.

"So..." Brynn swirls her orange juice around in her glass and then stares me down. "What's the deal with Braht? He went to your parents' cottage for Thanksgiving, right?"

"Right." That feels like a million years ago now.

"And what was that like?" Sadie asks.

"It was, um..." There is curiosity sparkling in their eyes. Both of them. Fucking girlfriends. "Okay, fine. It was orgasmic."

Sadie squeals and Brynn burps. But it's a happy, pregnant burp.

"Don't get excited, okay? That was just a one-time thing."

"You mean a two-time thing?" Brynn giggles. "Let's not forget the Hanky Panky Pantry."

"Shut up."

"Are you going to see him again?" Sadie asks.

"No!" I insist. Except that not seeing him is a big chore, since our desks align at work. Suddenly all my office supplies have developed a sex addiction. This morning I found my stapler and my tape dispenser in a compromising position. "I have a lot on my mind right now," I insist. And it's true.

"Oh, honey," Sadie says.

"We're here for you," Brynn echoes.

"I'm going to be fine," I say brightly. I put on my game face and smile. "Just fine!"

If only I believed that.

11 THE RETURN OF MAGNUM P.I.

Braht

All weekend I'm troubled by that phone call I took on Ash's line. When I gave her that message, she actually turned pale.

But then Ash made herself so scarce for the rest of the week that I wasn't able to ask her about it. I need to know what's got Ash's panties in a twist (besides me). But since I handed over that message slip, I can't follow up because I didn't save the number.

Obviously, desperate measures are called for.

There's this thing that action heroes do in movies when they need information. They take the *next* sheet in the memo pad and shade over it with a pencil's lead, revealing whatever was written on the previous page. I mean, I'm pretty sure I've seen Magnum P.I. do this countless times in re-runs. Or maybe it wasn't him? I just remember watching that show and thinking that his stache looked like it was eating his face.

Either way, I try this pencil rubbing thing with Ash's phone memo pad on Monday, and it works perfectly. When I use one of her expertly sharpened pencils to completely shade the page, the previous message is revealed! It reads:

Wine
Dumplings
Ice Cream
Wine

Damn it. Foiled again. And now I want ice cream.

I ponder my next move all morning (though I also show an adorable bungalow on Wilshire, because a man's gotta eat).

Monday afternoon I get my lucky break. Ash is out of the office again, but when her phone rings, my Spidey senses tingle.

Cockney Braht answers again. "Hello, matey! You've reached Ash Power's line at Ernst VanderMollen Realty. Can I be of service?"

"Ash, please," a man grumbles, and it's the same gruff voice. I didn't know I could hate a guy based on two words and a voice, but there you go.

"Whom shall I say is calling, good sir?"

"It's, uh, her friend John."

"You have a surname, John?"

"A what?"

Jesus. "A surname. A *lahst* name," I draw out the British pronunciation, just so he feels extra stupid. I suppose you aren't supposed to alienate the target of your investigation, but I can't help myself. Good thing the CIA never offered me a job.

"John Smith."

Really, dude? That's the best you can do? "What is your *numbah*, please."

The asswipe reads off a number that matches the caller ID on Ash's phone, and after promising to give Ash the message, I hang up on him.

Then I get to work.

My first Google search for a John Smith at that phone number reveals nothing. Of course it doesn't. So I try the number by itself. This is more promising. Ye olde Internet attributes that phone number to a Deborah Engersoll of Wyoming, Michigan.

So I google "Engersoll" and "Ashley Power" next.

My computer screen lights up with news stories. First there's Dwight Engersoll's arrest and indictment for embezzlement. Dwight Engersoll's prison sentence of five to seven years. I choose one of these articles and read it. Dwight was skimming money off Ash's former employer—a commercial real estate developer. At the time, Dwight worked for a software company that was hired to install accounting software at Ash's firm. That was his in.

White-collar crime makes for boring reading. Until I flip to the next page of search results, and that's where I find the bombshell: an old wedding announcement for one Ashley Power and Dwight Engersoll. According to the three lines of text, the happy couple eloped in Las Vegas when Ash was twenty-eight years old. And, if I've got the timeline right, he was arrested a mere seven months later.

My first thought is: *Oh, honey bear. You sure know how to pick 'em.*

My next thought is: *Why is he calling her now? And from where?*

Back to the search engine we go. I find the Michigan Department of Corrections database website and type in Engersoll. Ten seconds later I'm staring at his mug shot. I have to grudgingly admit that Mr. Dwight Engersoll takes a nice mug shot. It isn't a photo up to Bramly's standards, but the man looks surprisingly good for someone who's just been arrested. He has blondish hair and a face that's handsome in a smug sort of way.

The big flaw is his eyes, though. They're beady and mean. Also, Dwight Engersoll needs to get his eyebrows done. Seriously. They're like a couple of overgrown caterpillars. Real men manscape. I feel strongly about this.

Moving on.

Dwight's criminal record is laid out for my consumption. His first sentence was part of a plea deal. But then he reoffended in prison. There's a new conviction for *Controlled Substance: Intentional Manufacture or Distribution.*

Lovely. Embezzlement wasn't enough for him. He decided to peddle drugs in prison?

But the worst piece of information on this page is the last bit. Date paroled: October 5th.

Well, shit. My honey bear is dodging her twice-convicted ex-husband? And he's harassing her?

Goddammit. He needs to be held accountable. And by "held accountable" I mean "he needs to meet my fist in a parking lot at high noon." I am not above going a little Westworld on his ass.

Seriously. If he wants to get to Ash, he's going to have to go through me. And then he's going to the salon where he'll get tweezed. I'm going to make Unibrow suffer.

12 RED FLAGS AND TEQUILA

Ash

My smiley game face lasts at least five hours.

After brunch, I haul myself through the afternoon with a session at the gym. It's a good idea to get buff and feel strong when your ex-con ex is potentially stalking you, right? It kicks up the adrenaline and gets those fat-burning endorphins going.

Also, I deserve an exercise sticker.

Afterward, to remind myself that life is good, I follow up with a mani-pedi. Because hey—if my ex murders me for testifying against him, at least I'll die with a nice manicure.

Gallows humor. It's my new best friend.

I swing by my office at seven that evening, just to see what messages Braht might have taken for me. And—fine—I'm curious to see which of my personal belongings are having sex on my desk. That pencil sharpener has been aching for it, I'm sure.

The office is dark, and walking through the empty space creeps me out more than it really should. I didn't used to feel this way, like I'd been cast in a horror movie. If I happen to spot Pennywise or a red balloon ANYWHERE, I'm going to run in a heartbeat.

Sure enough, when I reach my desk I find that my staple puller is performing oral sex on my favorite pair of scissors. And there's a note in the middle of my desk blotter.

Honey bear, I'm a little worried about you. That same guy called again. I need to hear from you to make sure you're okay.

B-

Just like that, my blood pressure doubles. Dwight called the office again? He must be staying at his sister's house. And he wants something from me?

What the hell am I going to do?

Dwight knows where I work, and now I'm standing here in the empty office like a dummy.

Fuck!

I jam Braht's note in my pocket and head for the door. The heels of my suede ankle boots click impatiently as I make tracks for the rear exit. I press the lock bar and then push my way outside. The back lot smells like fall leaves, and I take a deep breath to steady myself. The sky is still streaked with light, but it's already quite dark back here. The trees make long shadows across the asphalt.

I am not creeped out. I am not creeped out. I am not...

I am totally creeped out!

And then someone steps out from the shadows as I approach my car, and I jump a foot into the air. At least.

"*Jesus*, Ashley. Easy," he says.

All the air leaves my lungs as I recognize Dwight's voice. I take him in with wild eyes. Even in bad light I can see that his hair is streaked here and there with gray. But everything else about him is...harder. And not in a good way. He looks...more broken, if that's possible. He's wearing a plain white T-shirt and jeans, instead of the suits he once favored. But that's not really it. It's his hardened expression that terrifies me.

"What do you want?" I ask in a shaky voice. I'm backing away.

The old Ashley is the one who'd back away; the new Ash stands firm!

Just not this time. I am backing away. I can't help it.

He lifts his hands in the air. "Just to talk, honey. I thought we could grab some dinner and catch up."

My jaw is hanging open now. It takes actual physical concentration to close it far enough that I can say, "Dwight, we are not old friends who haven't caught up in a while. You lied to me. You stole money from me. And I testified against you in court. We are *not going out to dinner!*"

As this monologue ends, he looks mildly affronted. "Drinks then? I know things ended badly, but we had some good times, too."

Good times? I'm shaking like a leaf right now. I don't know whether to run or kick him right in the *good times*. "Look. Don't contact me. Don't call my cell phone or my office. Just...lose my number." I say this while circling slowly, putting my body between Dwight and the driver's side of my car. He hasn't made a move toward me, but I'm still not okay.

I'm fucking terrified.

"I just wanted to..." he starts, but I am not listening anymore. My gut fauna is fucking on fire. Red flag! Red flag! Warning!

My hand plunges into my bag. I find my key and bleep the locks on my car. Then I turn and bolt for the driver's side door and jump in, slamming my finger down on the lock button as soon as I'm able. I tear into reverse and then wrench the car forward. He just stands there, and even though he's receding in my rearview mirror, he's still as big as life in my head.

The next few minutes are a shaky blur as I drive home on pure adrenaline. The car starts blasting Santana's *Supernatural* album, because hours ago I was in a brave (and obviously retro) kind of mood when I chose this music. But now "Put Your Lights On" hits too close to home.

I reach my street when I realize I may have just led Dwight right to my house. So I slide to a stop in front of a neighbor's house. I turn the music off and try to think. There aren't any headlights behind me, but I still feel scared.

This man took everything from me: my money, my reputation, my belief that men can be trusted.

I try to breathe. To think rationally and not react emotionally. The locked car is safe, so long as I never leave.

Wonderful.

The corners of my eyes prickle, and my throat gets hot. It's not like me to cry. It's not like me to panic, either. Quick! I need a consult. I touch Brynn's number on my phone, and she answers on the second ring.

"Hey baby!" she says, and I relax a little just at the sound of her voice. "You okay?"

"Yeah..." I say, shakily. *Please invite me over. Please.* "What's up with you tonight?"

"My lunch," she says with a sigh. "Today has been rough. So I'm just curled up on the couch with Tom, trying to keep saltines down while he rubs my feet. It's a pretty exciting night."

Oh boy. They're so cute it hurts a little. And I'll have to just let her be alone with her man. "You hang in there, okay?"

"Will do! Better go. Time to dry heave." I actually hear a gagging sound as she clicks off.

Ouch. Poor Brynn. I consider a call to Sadie next. But I can't really lay my troubles at her door right now. She's dealing with a lot. Besides, I think her sister has occupied her guest room.

Welp. Better make myself comfortable in my car. My eyes sting a little as I close them against the night. I take a deep breath and listen to the silence around me. This is the most strung out I've been for years. I know it's all my fault. I made bad choices when I was young and stupid. Hell, I wasn't even that young. I was just afraid to be alone. So I overlooked warning signs that shouldn't have been ignored.

Bad idea. I should have known it would come to this—hiding in my car from my vengeful ex, wondering what to do next.

This is a really safe block, though. My keys are in the ignition, so I'm ready to drive away if I have to. And it's so quiet that I'd hear another car coming down the silent road.

"*IT'S RAINING MEN!*" my phone shouts suddenly.

I leap about a foot, bang my thighs against the steering wheel, and drop the phone. I'm already a nervous wreck, so I'm positive something sinister has happened until I find the phone on the floor and turn it over.

The screen says, *Braht calling.*

That fucker changed my ringtone. I want to rip his bowels out with my bare hands. Lucky for him, I just got a new manicure. I swipe to answer, my finger shaking. "It's raining *men?*"

"Trust me, it's better than the first couple of ideas I had."

Then he chuckles warmly into my ear, and the golden sound of it brings my heart rate back under control. I'm a little less alone than I was a minute ago.

"What were the other ideas?" I ask, because I need to keep the conversation going, and to convince my heart rate to slow down. Right now, Braht is my lifeline, even if he doesn't know it.

"'I'm Too Sexy' would have been a good choice," he suggests.

I snort. "You flatter yourself."

"I was talking about you, baby."

"Smooth."

"Always."

There's a silence, but I can finally breathe again.

"Ash, you okay? We need to have a little chat about this guy who's called you twice. I know who he is."

"You *do?*" I look reflexively out of the car windows, checking the shadows beneath the streetlamp. But I don't see Dwight lurking anywhere.

"Yeah." His voice goes soft. "I hope you don't mind that I Googled the old news stories. I mean—I'm not a big fan of people Googling my past. But this felt like an emergency."

I try to take all that in. Braht has some kind of skeleton in his closet? In the back of my mind I think I knew that. It's about his family, though. Father? Grandfather? Someone was a criminal. I heard whispers at work. That's why he changed his last name.

But...now he knows about Dwight?

"You know about Dwight?" I squeak. "That he's out?"

"Parole decisions are public record, sugar pop."

I growl. Because *sugar pop*?

"What are you doing right now?" he asks.

"Just, uh, chillin." *Down the block from my house. In my car. Like a loser.*

"I'm making pulled-pork tacos. With fresh corn tortillas."

My stomach grumbles. "You cook?"

"Come over and see. You can tell me what you're doing about this ex-con who's trying to call you. And I can ply you with tequila and try to get your clothes off."

"Braht...!"

He chuckles into my ear, and it makes my damn nipples harden. "Just kidding with that last thing, although I could sure go for an Ash taco. Just making sure you were paying attention."

"If I come over, you have to be good." *Please be good*, I beg privately. I really need a friend right now.

"On my best behavior," he promises.

I hesitate for at least ten more seconds, because Braht's best behavior isn't really all that good. But tacos and companionship are calling more loudly than my conscience.

Also, my nipples tingle.

He gives me his address, and a minute later I'm driving toward East Grand Rapids, my stereo blaring confidently again.

13 MY FANTASY LIFE IS VERY DETAILED

Braht

Now, normally, when I'd have a foxy babe coming over, I'd do the normal routine: flip my collar up in a nod to the eighties, check my breath, do some push-ups to get my muscles popping, dim the lighting, spray some lavender (a much better aphrodisiac than Axe, my friend), and pour a couple of glasses of Lafite Rothschild or, you know, top-shelf vodka. Whatever the babe drinks.

But honestly, I haven't had a "foxy babe" over in forever because nobody has used that phrase since 1989. And I'm not planning on seducing Ash, because my Spidey sense is telling me that she's freaked out. And to take advantage of that would make me a Prime, Grade-A Asshole, and that's not me.

I'm Grade-A Prime, but not an asshole.

Besides, when the time is right, *she* can seduce *me*. When she's ready. In the meantime, there's always the shower, where I can lather up my cock, imagining it's *her* hand wrapped around my dick. It will have to do. For now.

So prepping for Ash's arrival is a little different. I put on a soft flannel shirt that's irresistible (organic cotton from Patagonia.

Raised by virgin monks in an untouched valley somewhere). My breath is fine (good hygiene). Lighting is bright and safe. Instead of lavender, the house smells of homemade cookies. (Oatmeal. The best kind.)

Back in the kitchen, I put on an apron. It was my grandmother's, and it has gingerbread dudes on it. I cut a couple of limes for margaritas.

Standing there at the counter, I allow myself the daydream of Ash coming home from work, finding me here waiting. I'm wearing the apron (but *only* an apron in my fantasy) to welcome her home. And plenty of skin and muscle to greet her. She's had a long day at work and I'm there to welcome her to our home. She swings the kitchen door open, her first sight is my bare ass. "Oh, baby," she says in a husky voice. "What's for dinner?"

"You're the appetizer," I answer. "Followed by me banging you on the countertop until your orgasmic screams bounce off the glass-tiled backsplash. Followed by chicken braised in wine and rosemary with garlic smashed potatoes, sesame green beans and a buttery white Bordeaux."

My fantasy life is very detailed. There will be lemon cake for dessert, with espresso. We'll need our energy for round two.

These good thoughts are interrupted by headlights in the driveway. I open the door, letting light spill out over the cobblestone path. I know Ash can see me, even if I'm only in silhouette. I turn and give a King Tut pose, because that's a surefire way to let her know it's me. I'm tempted to go to her and swoop her up in a big man-hug, but I've got to pace myself.

Step one: She's here.

Step ten thousand: She stays.

She turns off the headlights, turns off the car, and I'm a little surprised when she walks briskly up to me. And by briskly, I mean, she could compete in one of those walk-marathons, where you go toe-heel toe-heel. She's practically running. I open my arms to her, but she sidesteps me, walks inside, throws a huge bag on my couch and spins around.

"Did you make cookies or are you fucking with me?"

"Oatmeal. But you can't have one."

"Why?" Her skin is all flushed and her blonde hair is down and sorta wild looking. She's not a foxy babe. She's the *only* babe.

"Because it's for dessert. I promised dinner. Pulled pork tacos, remember? I've been pulling pork for at least an hour. It's exhausting and there's no release. I will make you a drink, though."

"I'm not doing shots with you. Or...pulling...*pork*. My clothes stay on," she says, and I'm glad to see that fight in her eyes again. Whatever spooked her is starting to slip away from her.

"I'll make you a margarita. On the rocks. And there's plenty we can do with our clothes on." I waggle my perfect eyebrows at her (no monobrow here—my stylist would be appalled).

She gives me a look that is pretty much like Cyclops in *X-Men* gives to unsuspecting enemies before he zaps the shit out of them. I am not unsuspecting, though. "Plenty of things we can do with our clothes on like...play Scrabble?"

She crosses her arms over her chest.

"Canasta?"

She actually harrumphs.

"Chick flick marathon?"

I see it in her eyes. I've got her number.

She says: "Okay. But I'll make the margaritas. You do the tacos."

She's angry even when she compromises. It's fucking adorable.

"Deal," I say. "Let me just tighten my apron, honey bear." I wink at her.

Ash

He fucking winks at me! I laugh a little, dammit, because I can't help it. Being around Braht is like being in front of a fire watching *Golden Girls* reruns. It's weirdly comforting, at least tonight.

He literally does keep that apron on. Who does that? At first I think it has cars on it, but when I look at it, his apron is peppered with little gingerbread men. And gingerbread women. And...are they doing it? No. It's just my sexually frustrated brain in action.

Braht knots that apron like he knows what he's doing. I'm not a cook. I'll admit that. It's why I always come running when Brynn calls. Well, it's not the only reason, I mean, I love her and all. But as I watch Braht work, I'm actually wondering if he could give her some competition. He's making corn tortillas from scratch.

I didn't even know that was possible. I thought corn tortillas were born that way, you know, flat and ready to fold.

I keep these thoughts to myself as I pour copious amounts of alcohol into a pitcher. Beside me, Braht turns lumps of some kind of masa mixture into food, flattening them out and cooking them on a hot griddle.

It's hard for me to admit, but he looks pretty adorable. I have a flash in my mind of him wearing that fucking gingerbread men apron with nothing under it, his arousal obviously pushing the apron up and out...

Hello, nipples. Nice to see you again.

I catch myself swaying to the music in the background. It's Buena Vista Social Club, because party boy Braht is the kind of guy who matches the tunes to his meal choice. He's humming to himself and the kitchen smells so good, and it's so...

Nice.

Just nice.

I grab two glasses, rub the edges with fresh lime, and dip them one at a time in margarita salt. Then I add ice to my amazing concoction. Braht's tortillas are ready to go. He's got some sliced radishes to garnish the pulled pork, farmers' cheese and what looks like fresh salsa. Holy hell, a girl could get used to this.

And by "a girl," I mean me.

I hand him a glass and say "Cheers," to which he says "Olé."
Fucking Braht.

After taking a sip, I realize that I'm not afraid anymore.

And this margarita is really good.

And I think Braht's apron is tenting just a little bit.

"Let's eat," he says, and I have to remind myself that he's
talking about the tacos.

We grab our plates and drinks and hunker down in front of his
massive leather couch, butts on the floor, plates on the coffee
table, backs against the sofa. He has about ten remote controls.
"Are you serious?" I say.

"Hey, don't knock it. Those have serious firepower. One of
them could even give you an orgasm."

He grabs one off the table, presses a series of buttons, and
then his window blinds begin to roll down. The music stops. The
TV flicks on.

"Don't dim the lights," I say as a fresh flash of fear shoots
through me. I'm not afraid of Braht making the moves on me. I'd
tell him to fuck off, but honestly, I just don't want to be in the
dark right now. My mind keeps going back to the parking lot and
Dwight and all the things that could've happened but thankfully
didn't.

"No lighting changes," he promises. The TV menu pops up.
"What are you in the mood for?" He starts scrolling. "*Jeopardy?*
Horror movies? Sci-fi?" Before I can answer, he says "Oh!
Moonstruck. God, I love this movie."

He presses enter and there's Cher and Nicolas Cage in a
kitchen. I don't think I've ever watched this movie all the way
through. It's old. I've heard good things about it, and it was pre-
mullet and pre-douchebag Nicolas Cage, but still. I'm not sure I
can suspend my disbelief long enough to buy him as a romantic
lead, especially in the eighties. "Is Nicolas Cage supposed to be
sexy here, because I'm really not..."

"SHHHHH!" Braht says. "This is the best part." He whispers
that and I look over to see if he's serious. He has one taco poised

halfway to his mouth, frozen in midair, and his other hand is latched onto my knee. What the...?

I'm not sure what's happening onscreen now, but it's something about Nicholas Cage having lost his hand and Cher getting hit by a bus. Then Cage grabs her, kisses her, she slaps him, she kisses him, and he carries her to the bed.

We watch it in devoted silence. It takes a little bit of pulled pork falling to the floor from Braht's taco to break the spell. I mean, that scene is fucking hot.

I shake it off. "I don't know why I'm surprised, but I never took you for liking chick flicks."

"What do you mean?"

"This is totally a chick flick."

He sets his taco down and turns to me as if this is really important. "*Moonstruck* is not a chick flick. It's a brilliant classic film about love and longing. And there's an amazing monologue where Ronny talks about losing his hand and how everyone else still has a hand...and I can just relate. To the not-having-a-hand part and really wanting a hand. It's one of my favorite movies." Then he returns to his taco. It's gone in two bites. Two.

"Name your other favorite movies," I challenge him.

"All of them?" He chugs his margarita.

"Hmm. Top ten? Top five?"

"That's totally easy," he says. Somehow I've gotten closer to him on the floor. When he sits back, I actually snuggle in beside him. He's wearing a ridiculously soft shirt that feels good against my skin. And I watch with fascination as he ticks off the names of films on his fingers. "*When Harry Met Sally. The Devil Wears Prada. Roman Holiday. Clueless.* And *Working Girl.*"

I burst out laughing. I can't help it. "Those are *all* chick flicks. You should just hand over your man card right now."

"Not a chance." Braht's expression grows intense. "In the first place, I gave you a very thorough demonstration of my man card last week. I don't remember hearing any complaints."

I swallow hard, because this is certainly true.

"And secondly, you're looking at this all backward."

"I...am?" And why can't I look away? He has the most beautiful, intelligent eyes.

"Yeah, you are," he whispers. "It's the guy who has a firm grip on his man card that can hold your purse. He's not afraid to be seen with that Tory Burch you like to carry—nice color, by the way. He'll free up your hands because he *likes* your hands, and he remembers all the terrific things you can use them for."

"Oh," I say slowly. Now my fingers itch to reach out for him. I have to make fists with both hands so I won't do it.

"Furthermore, he's not afraid to quote *Working Girl*. Because Joan Cusack is a genius. And who wouldn't want to say Melanie Griffith's best line out loud?"

I can't help saying it with him, and together we sound like the world's horniest Greek chorus: "*I have a head for business and a body for sin.*"

Sin sounds pretty good right now, actually. But Braht's not done with his speech. "Any man who tells you that chick flicks are for pussies can't be any good in bed. Because that man does not speak the language of women. He doesn't know that a little luxury can erase a shitty day of worrying about your ex..."

Braht takes my hand in his and begins to massage it. He has a great technique, applying gentle pressure between each joint. I relax just a little bit more against him.

"...That man doesn't speak the language because he's afraid of sounding like a girl. But fuck that noise, honey bear. If a man doesn't have the vocabulary to describe a satin teddy with peekaboo lace and mother-of-pearl snaps at the crotch, he can't buy it for you and then strategically ask you to wear it. He can't plan ahead to blow your mind sometime by lifting your skirt somewhere semi-public and dangerous. And he can't get down on his knees and kiss that lace and then pop open those snaps while you bite your own hand to keep from screaming when you climax." Braht takes a deep breath and lets it out in one hot gust. "Fuck. What was the point of this speech?"

"Um..." My voice is hoarse, and my face is suddenly very hot. Let's not even mention my nipples. "Man cards, I think." But I'm not sure, because everything tingles.

"Right," he says with a sigh. "Still got mine. Shall we watch *Working Girl* next?"

"Okay," I breathe, sinking a little further into his comforting embrace.

Braht aims the most enormous remote control at the television and pushes some buttons. That Carly Simon anthem floods his top-notch surround sound system, and my heart races in a good way.

Braht turns his head and gives me a quick kiss on the jaw. Even that paltry contact makes me crazy. I want to rip all his clothes off him and climb on his dick.

But we're not doing that tonight. I can't send this man any more mixed signals. So I watch the movie instead.

Nine hours later I'm face down in heaven. Braht has super-silky sheets and premium feather pillows.

Of course he does.

Last night I purposely drank too many margaritas so I couldn't safely drive back home. Braht tucked me into one of his guest rooms to sleep it off.

Now I'm vaguely aware that morning has arrived. There have been showering sounds and coffee smells. But I can't get up. This is the most relaxed I've been since finding out that my ex is out of prison, because my subconscious knows that I'm safe and hidden in a house where Dwight can't find me.

My subconscious likes this turn of events a lot. I might need another three hours of sleep just to break even. Also, I'm in and out of a terrific dream. Something about lingerie that snaps open at the crotch, and a willing tongue.

The mattress shifts, and the edge of the bed dips gently. A warm hand palms my back.

More, my subconscious begs. *Touch me.*

"Wake up, sugar pop," a voice says. "We have a meeting."

"No," I grumble. I don't like meetings. And that hand isn't doing what I need it to do. "Lower. Hand."

There's a chuckle. "I wish." The hand leaves me.

Braht's voice?

Fuck! I flip over and sit up fast. "Hi!" I gasp. I think I just asked him to grope me. Did that happen?

"Hi yourself. Here's your coffee." He lifts a mug from the bedside table. "Open those pretty eyes all the way. We have a new gig."

"What?" I'm still trying to navigate a thick fog born of both sleepiness and embarrassment. "Gig? Who?"

"Our thriller writer who bought Tom's house? She's putting hers on the market."

"A new listing?" That snaps me to consciousness. "Where is it?"

"On the back side of Reed's Lake. Google Earth shows a really small roofline. Could be hard to price. Drink up." He presses the coffee cup into my hand. For one split second, his gaze slips. His eyes travel downward over my scantily clad body. "Rawrrr," he meows.

"Stop it," I say. "You're making me giggle, and I don't like giggling."

"How can you not like giggling?"

I walk past Braht sipping this amazing coffee that I'm pretty sure he made with a real espresso machine. "Giggling chafes," I say and I head for the shower.

"Hey!" Braht says, and I feel his hand on my elbow. I consider leaning back, my ass pressed up against him. But then he says, "What's this, a tattoo?"

His hand moves down my back to my panty line, and suddenly everything in me goes cold. I mean, I freeze from the inside out.

"Nothing," I say, the words sharper than necessary. I tug my panties a half inch lower, hoping it covers it up. I'd tried to have that tattoo removed ages ago, but some things you just can't make disappear.

It's faded now, but the memory of my worst mistake never will.

14 BLACK CAT AND AN OCTOBER CONFESSION

Ash

"Do we even want this listing?" Braht asks me as Ms. T.S. Archer drives away in her Mercedes. We watch her tail lights recede. "I feel like this is some kind of shakedown."

"It will be fine," I insist, because arguing with Braht is in my blood. "You're worried about your manicure, aren't you?"

Braht gives me an arch look. "I was worrying about *yours*, honey bear. Because I know you'll get pissy if I do more than my share of the work."

He has a point. I need to pull my own weight, and this won't be easy. T.S. Archer—and let's be honest for a second, the woman's name is plain old Tracy—has not taken such great care of her delightful little property on the lake. Apparently thriller-writing is an engrossing pastime, because the garden hasn't been tended to for months. The lawn is practically a meadow. Ivy has taken over the brick facade. The effect would be picturesque but the vines are actually threatening the front door.

Maybe thriller writers need a lot of atmosphere. I can picture a tendril of ivy wrapped around a butcher knife, poised to stab me *Psycho*-shower-scene-style.

Before she left us, the seller had said: "The listing is yours...*if* you can feed my cat and tidy up the yard while I'm in Cuba."

Braht and I didn't even need to look at each other. We just nodded in tandem. Nobody turns down a waterfront listing. Even if it's going to take us days to make the place presentable.

Even if she just conned us into free cat-sitting.

Now she's off to the airport while Braht and I try to figure out how we've been suckered into cleaning up her mess.

"At least the interior is in good shape," I say, searching for some good news. I'm totally wearing the wrong clothes for yard work. My silk blouse, pencil skirt and stilettos are not conducive to weed-pulling.

"It's in *okay* shape," Braht hedges. "Do you think we should market the place as a teardown? It needs a second bathroom almost as badly as I need two fingers of Macallan 18 year. Be a dear and run out for whisky?"

"You know it's only eleven thirty in the morning, right?" I don't know where all his negativity is coming from.

"I *hate* being taken advantage of," he grouses. "I'm always cleaning up after other people."

He actually sounds upset. Like, this is Braht with a real human emotion.

"She's a helpless old lady!" I say firmly. *With great bargaining skills*. I totally respect that.

"She's a con artist!" I don't think I've ever seen him so grumpy.

"We just earned a bunch of money off her purchase, though. And we can always outsource the landscaping. Calm down, okay? This is merely a bump in the road, sugar butt."

Braht startles at my use of one of his ridiculous nicknames. "You're teasing me." He sounds both surprised and impressed.

"Like it's hard." I just had my first good night's sleep in days, and it's fun to turn the tables on him for once. "Go find that wheelbarrow she mentioned. Let's just see how much we can get done in a couple of hours."

Not enough, it seems.

By five o'clock, Braht's irritation is contagious. I want to tell T.S. Archer where she can shove her overgrown flowerbeds and her unraked leaves. My hands are dirty and scratched. My feet hurt. And worst of all, my manicure is trashed.

The only perk is the view. I'm not talking about the one on Reed's Lake. Braht's been slowly removing pieces of his clothing since we began working. First the jacket and tie. Then his belt and dress shirt. He's wearing a pair of jeans he found in the back of his car. I'm wearing the sweatpants and T-shirt he removed from his gym bag for me, unfortunately still in heels.

The clothes Braht gave me smell like him. I've spent the day trying not to notice. Now we're covered in dirt and only halfway done, and I'm absolutely starving.

"Okay, I'm calling it," I say, tossing another handful of desiccated lily stalks into the wheelbarrow. "That is enough for one day. Let's feed the cat and get out of here. We need food. And a shower."

He grunts in agreement. "Who could sit down to dinner with dirt under his nails? It's barbaric."

I'm sure his friend Tom gets plenty dirty in his line of work. I don't point this out, because Braht's been in a mood all day. "I'll handle the kitty. Back in a jif."

Inside the house, everything is still. Slowly I take another walk around the space. The house is too small, and the footprint is very 1960s. But there are lake views from most of the rooms.

And except for an abundance of cat hair, there's nothing out of place. Ms. Archer must be a fan of those TV shows where they show you how to style a home for a quick sale. There's no clutter. She's already removed all the detritus of everyday life—the bottles of lotion, the stray pennies, the unpaid bills. The countertops and tables are empty except for a few carefully placed items—like the photography book in the center of the desk.

The effect is classy. She's even left an arrangement of red roses in a vase on a living room table. They look terrific against the lake in the distance and the autumn leaves outside.

According to the instructions I've pocketed, I open a can of cat food and plop the stinky stuff into the empty bowl. "Here, kitty kitty kitty!" I call.

A black streak runs into the room from the back of the house somewhere, butting my shin out of the way and diving at the bowl.

"Where are your manners?" I gasp, just to amuse myself. The cat turns its head and glares at me out of its one remaining eye.

The thriller writer has a black, one-eyed cat. Of course she does.

"See ya, puss. Stay out of trouble." I leave it alone to eat in peace.

My cell phone rings. Braht must be getting impatient out there. He's so moody right now. So I press answer and bark "What?"

But then I hear *him* breathing. And I *know*. There's a sudden crash behind me and I jump about a foot.

Fucking cat. Please let it just be the cat.

"Come on, Ash..." Dwight's voice is low and scary. "You ran away from me last night, and that's not nice. You need to listen to me. All I want from you..."

I hit end call, my hands shaking uncontrollably. And I can't get outside to Braht fast enough.

BRAHT

Okay, fine. I'm in a bad mood. Men can have moods, too.

I try some deep breathing exercises that I've learned from my meditation coach, but it doesn't help. Even alternate nostril breathing doesn't calm me. It just gets me even more pissed that I can't breathe out of both my nostrils and find my zen.

How long does it take to feed a cat? I could birth a cat in the amount of time Ash has been in there.

Yes, I'm aware that I'm not making a lick of sense.

I take a real breath and laugh a little bit, because clearly, I'm not myself. Why the hell am I stretched taut, like a guitar string pulled too tightly? I'm ready to snap at just one touch.

I know why, though. It's a rare form of PTSD that occurs whenever someone gives me the runaround.

I'm only half joking about the PTSD.

When I was seventeen, I came home to an abandoned house, littered with the evidence of a frenzied move. My parents had made a hasty escape, leaving three things for me to deal with: their mess, their debt, and my brother. Their choice was to abandon their kids or end up in jail.

But it took me a while to understand what was really happening. There was a note and an envelope on the kitchen table:

Sebastian—

We're having a crisis, so we need you to be a man and help us solve it. Your father's business has hit some trouble and we need to do some banking overseas. Here's $500 for the things you'll need until we come back for you.

This is important—you must not tell a soul that we're out of town. The only way this works is if we take care of business and then send plane tickets for you and Bramly. But if you let on that you two are on your own right now, the social workers will take you both into custody before we can fix this.

We know we can count on you, son.

Love,

Mom

I did what she asked. For five weeks I kept everything together without telling anyone. Bramly was only twelve and distraught at this turn of events, so I spent much of the time comforting him.

Then, finally, I picked up the phone one day and heard, "Sebastian? Is that you?"

"Mom?" My voice choked up immediately. For a month I'd been pushing away my own fear, trying to earn my man card the way she wanted me to. But when she finally called I couldn't take it anymore. "Are you coming home now?" I asked, ending the question with an embarrassing sob.

"Sebastian, stop that. Listen. It's not safe for us to come home. We want to, but we'd end up in jail. And that's no better for you than if we're hiding in Europe."

Hiding in Europe? My eighteen-year-old brain couldn't even make sense of that. Except... "We keep getting calls," I told her. "Dad's investment partners have stopped by the house looking for him."

"You have no idea where we are," my mother said quickly.

That was a hundred percent true.

"And we never had this conversation. I called to tell you that it's going to take some more time."

"What is?"

"Your plane tickets. Well—your brother's, anyway. You're heading to college, so you don't really need us. I would take Bramly, but he doesn't even have a passport. And I can't come home to get him one. In a couple of months we'll figure this out."

"M-months?" I stuttered.

She made more excuses and then hung up on me, telling me to hang in there.

Over the next two weeks, I eventually figured out what happened. Dad had helped himself to a lot of his investors' money, stashing it in Swiss bank accounts. When his actions were about to be discovered, he and my mother had left the country.

Maybe they really did think they could keep the family together in Europe. Or maybe not. But I turned eighteen and filed for custody of Bramly. When the FBI came calling, I realized I'd helped my parents escape by not speaking up sooner. Horrified, I cooperated with them.

I never heard from our parents again, and neither did Bramly. They chose their liberty and their stolen cash over their kids. A part of me will never get over it.

Fast forward almost twenty years and there's something about this listing that pushes my buttons. The way the little old lady took off, leaving us to deal? It's giving me agita.

If Ash would just climb into the car with me, I'd feel better. I know I would. She soothes an ache I didn't even know I had. Finally the door opens, and she emerges from the house in a hurry. I watch helplessly as she stumbles and almost falls. It's those fucking shoes. She looks amazing in them, but they've been giving her trouble all day.

I imagine cradling her feet in my lap later, rubbing out the knots, my hands moving up her calves...

I'm already breathing easier.

Until she jumps in the car and says "Go! Go! Go!" I don't even really process her words, I just floor it in reverse and then speed out of the driveway. I see a flash of eyes in the window...or make that I see a flash of a cat's eye (single) in the window and I get it. "Not a cat person?" I ask once we're safely down the driveway and speeding into downtown, surrounded by street lights flicking on. A light rain starts to fall. I turn on the windshield wipers and the rhythmic thunking is sort of calming.

"Something like that," she breathes. Then she says, "Braht..."

There's something about the way she says my name. I don't even have a cocky response to her right now. Something's not right with her, and I want to help her. I need to help her.

"Yeah?"

"Can you just take me home?"

"Of course," I say, feeling, I'll admit, a little disappointed that we won't be having dinner together.

I turn the car around, thoughts of taking her out for wine and tapas abandoned. She's had her hair in a ponytail, but she pulls on the band and shakes her hair out. I get a quick whiff of her shampoo. I try to focus on driving.

"Can you maybe talk a little bit?" she asks.

"Talk?"

"Yeah. I just need you to..." She takes a deep breath. "Talk to me. Give me some Braht chatter. About whatever is on your mind. The luxury car you want next, or your golf swing. Anything."

"Why is that, honey bear?" The rain is beating down now, and I slow the car. Safety first. Also, I want to prolong my time with her.

"Just need to hear your voice."

I chuckle, but I'm so conflicted. She needs me, but she won't ever come out and say how much. "We can't both have a meltdown today, okay? Let's arm wrestle for it. Winner gets to have the panic attack. Loser buys the tequila."

She makes a soft little noise of surprise. "I'm sorry. I'm such a jerk. I noticed that earlier—that you weren't okay. What happened to you back there at the house? Something switched. And it scared me a little." Her voice is so small, so un-Ash-like that my heart shivers a bit.

"No," I backpedal. "I'm fine. I was simply hungry."

"Bullshit. You weren't you. Or maybe that *is* the real you. I just need to know."

The word *need* echoes inside my chest for a moment. I don't know if telling Ash my story is the right thing to do. But I'm not good at saying no to her.

My hands feel twitchy on the steering wheel. I never tell this story. I don't like to think about it. And Ash is too silent on her side of the car.

"My parents just...left Bramly and me when we were younger."

"Left you?"

"Yup. They thought they had better things to do than raise their kids. Bramly was twelve... And they left us with nothing." I don't want to describe my parents' fraudulent activities because I don't like admitting that I was too stupid to figure out that they were using me to help them escape the country.

Besides, everyone in Western Michigan already knows that part of the story. I'm sure Ash has heard it at some point. My father's name was in the papers for months. Though my name and Bramly's name were always omitted, probably because we were so young.

Small mercies. But I changed my name after college even so.

"Anyway, I know our thriller writer can't actually leave me destitute, but when people dump their bullshit on my doorstep I get stabby."

"They *left you?*" Her voice is all high and weird.

"Yeah. No food in the fridge. No money in the bank. No note from Mommy for their tearful sixth grader." It's really a wonder my brother is a semi-functional human. "I managed to stay in the house for a couple of months before the bank took it." Or maybe it was the feds. At the time, all I knew was that we were in trouble. "And then I was awarded custody of my brother and I had to start from scratch."

"But...you drive an Audi," she says. "You have marble countertops." She's trying to do the math. "You dress like the Poster Boy for the Rich and Powerful."

I laugh at that. Must be all the pastel plaids. "Sometimes," I tell her. "But I've earned what I have. It's taken almost two decades, but it's just hard work."

There's one more thing I want to add, but I can't seem to voice it. But it's this—no matter what I do, or how much I earn, I know I'll never be enough. Not for my parents...and maybe not for Ash. But I can't say that, so I make a joke. "My good looks, my endless charm, and huge dick are just gifts I was born with...but everything else I have because I fought for it."

She's quiet. A quiet I can't read. Maybe the joke didn't work. (Though, let's face it, I'm huge.)

"I just wanted you to know," I add, lamely.

We've reached her place. The rain is coming down harder, and I know it will pull all the fall color off the trees. I feel the same way—like I've been drained of color. I shouldn't have said anything to Ash. It's better for people to think you're a god than to know you're human.

Why would she want me now? Fuck. I've screwed up. She's going to think I'm a loser.

That's when a miracle happens. She unlatches her seat belt, leans over and she kisses me.

Ash.

Kisses. Me.

Her lips are soft, warm and inviting. I don't dare breathe. I don't move. I don't think I can.

"Will you walk me to the door?" she asks.

I don't have to say anything. She already knows I will.

Ash

As I let myself into the house, I'm still a little shaky. From the phone call, yes, but also from what Braht told me. It's like my entire worldview has shifted, or at least my worldview of him has shifted. I was thinking he was too good to be true. And I was right—he's *better*.

He walks me to my door and I don't know what possesses me. Maybe the kiss in the car? The way he looks like a sad little boy right now. Or maybe it's just that I don't want to be alone. "Look," I say. "I'm starving and you've got to be, too. You want to order some takeout? And just hang out? Eat? Decompress?" *Or*, I think, *I can help you shower and we can wash the bad day and bad memories off and be all wet and slippery*. I clear my throat because *ahem*.

Braht just says, "Hell, yes," and walks inside.

I wonder what he thinks of my space. Like my desk at work, it's carefully coordinated. Everything is white. I like things sleek and bright. There's no clutter. I have a few plants here and there because living things help with balancing out bad juju.

"What are you hungry for?" he asks, and I almost blurt *You.*

"Pizza?" I say instead. There's something immensely comforting about warm and gooey pizza on a cold, dark and rainy night.

"I'll call. You shower," he says, almost as if reading my mind.

I kick off my heels on the way out of the room. They're a lost cause now, all scuffed and battered from today. Then I peel off the sweats Braht loaned me and toss them in the hamper. It's a shame I have to give them back. I can kinda see myself lounging around in them on the weekend, my head in Braht's lap, flipping through a magazine.

Gah! I've got to knock that shit off now. The last thing I need is any part of my body in his lap. I need to focus, deal with Dwight, and move on.

I raise the window a few inches because the ventilation can't keep up with my ten-minute-shower habit. Then I turn on the water. While it heats, I unhook my bra. I drop my panties, and then allow my fingers to linger on the skin of my bottom, on the spot that drew Braht's eye this morning. The tattoo has faded over time. I don't even know if it's legible anymore. It's just a series of numbers. Dwight had asked me to prove my love for him, so I'd tattooed our anniversary onto my ass.

Yes, my ass. What can I say? I was making all kinds of Poor Life Choices. It seemed romantic then. Now, it's just a reminder of my many deep regrets. I could probably have it lasered off or at least covered over, but now I keep it as a reminder of how not to live. Letting a man take control of my life? It's never happening again.

Also, it's on my butt. So unless someone like Braht happens to spot it, I can usually forget it's there.

The shower is amazing. The hot water sluicing over me wipes all the grime off and eases my aches. Ten minutes later (okay, fine, it's more like fifteen) I emerge clean and buffed and ready for anything.

And by anything, I mean I'm ready for pizza and Braht, maybe not in that order.

I'm toweling off, thinking happy thoughts, when I open the window a couple more inches. I need to dry my hair, and it's still like a rainforest in here.

I start the brushing process at the ends of my hair and work upward. A girl can't rush the brushing process. That leads to split ends and that way lies the abyss. Braht is probably impatient with me already. But maybe he's sitting in my living room enjoying his first slice of pizza.

We really should have discussed the toppings beforehand. I'm a little nervous to know what Braht likes on his pizza. If he leans toward Hawaiian style, I'll have to rethink my attraction to him.

I'm debating the merits of pepperoni versus meatball when movement outside the window catches my eye. It takes a second to zero in on it, because the object I've noticed is black, and it's not easy to pick out against rain-dampened tree trunks in the dusk. There's a seven-foot fence that runs along the back of my tiny yard. The fence is what keeps the house private from the wooded bike trail that runs along behind my property.

Or it's supposed to. But now an object has risen above the fence level and is peering at me through the gloom. A black box with a shiny round eye, like a giant bug's. "Holy shit," I breathe. Because any girl who's ever binged on a James Bond movie marathon can identify a spy camera when she sees one. She also understands why polyester will never come back in style.

I close my eyes and let out a scream that's worthy of a slasher movie. It's epic, and I actually scare myself a little with my volume.

About three seconds later the bathroom door flies open. "Ash! Jesus! Is there a spider?"

As if I could be frightened by something as insubstantial as a spider. I jab my finger toward the window and watch as Braht's gaze turns in that direction. He grabs a magazine and rolls it up, ready to pounce.

"Um, what's the matter?" he asks.

I look out the window again and see nothing at all except wet trees and a good, solid fence. "A camera," I blurt. "Above the fence. It was just there. It was black. Pointy. James Bondish."

Braht takes two steps, pushing past me. "Nice towel," he says as he shoves the window open wider. "Is that Garnet Hill? Eileen Fisher?"

I don't even get a chance to answer because he puts one foot on the toilet and then *leaps to the ground below*, rolled-up magazine in hand. I'm not sure what he plans to do with it. Slap the peeping Tom? Show him what's on sale?

A squeak of surprise escapes my throat. That window isn't even very big. I hear footsteps hustling outside, and I stick my head out to see Braht disappearing around the edge of the fence. Then he's out of view for a few minutes. I throw on my bathrobe and wait for any sign of him.

Time passes slowly, and I spend it pacing between the bathroom and my living room. I'm a little freaked out and basically showing the world my bathrobe cleavage every time I walk into the bathroom. So I close the window and wait for Braht.

And wait.

He is coming back, right? Should I be calling the cops right now? What if he's lying battered and bloody on the bike path, the victim of a serial killer who spies on women before he claims them?

Or maybe he found that asshole Dw...

I can't even think my ex's name or something terrible will happen. I know it. And a black one-eyed cat crossed my path today, too. Anything could happen.

Just as I'm working myself back up into a lather, the front

door opens and Braht steps inside, magazine no longer in his hands. It's simply gone. "Honey bear?"

"I'm not your honey bear," I say automatically, but with no annoyance. It's a reflex.

He ignores that. "I couldn't find anything."

"No?" The camera I saw was substantial, and it was obviously raised above the fence by a tall...stick? Or by someone on a ladder? "Did you go behind the fence?"

"I did. I swear. Whoever you saw was gone." He makes a slight grimace. "There wasn't a soul back there. It's wet and dark. Not exactly a great time to bike or run. But, seriously—location, location, location. Well done, savvy buyer."

"Thank you." My shoulders slump. "I'm sure I saw a camera. It was looking right at me." At least I think I saw it.

Fuck.

"I'm *sure* you did," Braht says, but his tone suggests that my sanity may be fragile. "Let's eat, okay?"

I pull my robe a little tighter and glance out of the living room window. Only a square of blackness looks back at me. Anyone could be standing out there, staring inside. I hurry over to the front window and yank the curtains closed.

"Ash," Braht says softly. "If someone is spying on you in the bathroom, I don't know if you should stay here tonight."

"I don't know, either," I admit. Either I'm being stalked or I'm paranoid to the point of hallucination. I really don't like either option very much. I clutch my robe more tightly against my breasts, feeling eyes on me even though the drapes are already shut.

Braht's face softens. "Hey, baby duck. It's going to be okay. If that was your ex, spying on you is probably a parole violation. Should we call the cops? You could start building a case that he's stalking you, and nail him to the wall."

Stalking. The word lodges itself in my throat, and then burns. I'm being stalked. I have a stalker. My eyes get hot.

"Aw." Braht makes a clicking sound. He takes two steps closer and pulls me against his chest. He smells like fresh air and fall leaves.

I burrow into his neck and take a deep, steadying breath. I'm not a crier, damn it. And I won't let Dwight turn me into one.

15 HOW TO RESPOND TO A THREAT: WITH PIZZA & FACIALS

Braht

Ash is hugging me like I'm her long-lost teddy bear, and I like it. A lot. But I have to interrupt this hug for an important question. "Will you let me call the police?"

"Fuck no."

"Why not?"

She removes her head from my shoulder. "Because I'll sound like an insane person? *Hey, I saw a camera. And then it vanished into the mist. Do something.* We're not calling them. It will take hours, and they'll just nod and treat me like a paranoid chick."

I wince because she's probably right. So I fold like an underdone soufflé. "Okay, hon. We can skip that step for now on one condition. If you see your ex at all, you'll tell me. Or *anything* weird."

"Okay."

"And you're staying at Casa Braht until this fucker learns a lesson."

"Okay," she says again.

"And you'll wear nothing but lingerie when I'm home.

Preferably edible." I give her a cheesy wink so she'll know I'm only kidding.

I get an eye roll, which is actually helpful. On most people, you should check their pulse. But with Ash, I check for sass. If she can't tell me to fuck off, then it's time to dial the paramedics.

"Then pack a bag so we can move on to the dinner-eating portion of this evening."

I watch Ash stalk into her bedroom on those long legs of hers. She takes out a duffel bag and throws a bunch of clothes into it. She zips it shut.

"Well done! Let's go eat."

"Patience, I'm not done," she says. "It's a lot of work to look this fashionable all the time."

I'm too nice to point out that she's wearing a terry cloth robe that says HILTON on the front, and not much else.

A second suitcase emerges from beneath the bed. She opens a drawer and begins tossing some underwear into it.

"Can I choose the lingerie?" I ask, just to uphold my reputation.

"Not a chance."

"Can I choose the pizza toppings?"

She looks at me and I think she's actually considering it. Then she says: "You can have veto power."

Oh, Ash. You're such a badass and I love it.

When I've tossed her bag into the back seat of the car, and tucked Ash into the passenger's seat, I slide in behind the wheel and start the car.

Then I make a call while I wait for my baby to warm up. (The car, not Ash. I'll warm her up later.)

"Yo! How's the Brahtwurst?" Tom's voice booms through the sound system when he answers the phone. It's like he's all around us, like Zeus or something.

"You're on speaker, and there's a lady present," I tell him.

"I meant you, not your dick. But feel free to catch me up on either one," he says. And then there's a deafening guffaw.

Guffaws are real. I never believed it until I met Tom.

"Listen," I say. "Ash has had a shitty day. I'm going to take her to Casa Braht and ply her with beer and pizza. But I think she'd like to have her girls around her." I do a quick look to Ash and she nods, a slight smile lifting the corners of her mouth. "Can you send Brynn and Sadie over to cheer her up? I didn't have Brynn's number, but since you two are attached at the hip these days I knew I could just call you." I pull away from the curb and head down the street.

There's a silence on the line. "Ash is with you? Like, willingly?"

"Well, I haven't restrained her, if that's what you're asking. But we are in a moving vehicle."

"Wow," Tom says.

"Hi, Tom," Ash says, trying to sound upbeat, but I can hear the tension underneath.

"Hey, Ash. Sorry you're having a shitty day," he says.

"Thanks."

"I'll send Brynn over to Braht's. She isn't feeling very pukey tonight, so she'll probably be pretty happy to see you, honey."

"I'll be happy to see her, too."

"How come he's allowed to call you honey and I'm not?" I wonder aloud.

"Because I'm not a super sleaze who's always trying to get in her pants?" Tom booms.

"Huh. I suppose that could be it," I concede.

"Later, Tom!" Ash calls.

"Later, baby." He clicks off.

Baby. I kind of want to punch my best friend for calling Ash baby. And he called her honey. You put that together and you've got honey-baby and something weird happens in my gut. I'm the only one that should call her honey baby.

"Honey baby," I mumble.

"Huh?" I'm not sure if she's answering me or if she didn't hear me.

So yeah.

I've got it bad.

Brynn doesn't just show up, she mobilizes the forces. We've barely arrived at my manse and ordered the pizzas when she and Sadie walk through the door. Brynn is carrying a grocery bag. She's also wearing these weird terrycloth wristbands. "Are you training for something?" I ask.

"Yep. Pregnancy," she says.

I don't understand, but I nod anyway. I take the grocery bag from her. "I ordered dinner," I say. "Dare I hope that bag is full of alcoholic beverages?"

"There's beer. But mostly I come bearing supplies for a killer organic facial."

"Facial?" Ash perks right up.

"You betcha," Brynn says, marching past her. "Sadie! Cut up the pineapple."

"We bought pineapple *chunks*," Sadie argues. "It's already cut."

"Oh, perfect," Brynn says.

"Oh yummy," I add.

"It's for our faces," Sadie snaps.

Where have these women been all my life? "My skin loves pineapple just as much as the next guy."

Brynn halts in her tracks and looks me up and down. "Tom is over at Sadie's right now, watching sportsball on the couch. You could join him if you want."

"And miss the facials?"

There is an awkward silence while Brynn and Sadie stare at me through slitted eyes, and I'm pretty sure I'm about to be booted out of my own home.

"He's not making fun of you," Ash puts in. "The dude will

totally do facials with us. I'm pretty sure his manicure is fresher than mine."

"See?" I offer my hands as proof. They're short, buffed, and clean, in spite of the yard work I did today.

"Well then," Brynn says, sounding a little impressed. "Braht, open the beer and find four towels."

I do what I'm told, because I know a good thing when I see it.

An hour later I'm lying on the floor of the den, my feet propped up onto the Italian leather couch. I'm slightly drunk and full of pizza. My pores have been steamed open with pineapple water and are now slathered with some sort of fresh-smelling avocado goo. There are cucumber slices covering my eyes.

Brynn called it a masque treatment. Masque with a Q, not a K. Because mask with a K is too downmarket for this extravagance I'm experiencing. Various things were rubbed onto my face and now everything is cool and pleasantly tingly.

"This is the besht," Sadie slurs next to me. She's had three beers already. And since she's about 5'2 and a hundred pounds, that seems like plenty.

"It is," I agree. Although mashing avocados and then not eating them seems a bit like a sacrilege. A little lime and garlic with some chips... "Do you feel less stressed?" I ask Sadie, to keep up my end of the conversation.

"Sorta. Did you know my husband is cheating on me with the nanny?"

"I didn't," I admit. What do you say to that? I opt for the truth. "I'm sorry. In fact, I apologize for all stupid men. I can't imagine why that seemed like a good idea."

"Because I didn't lose the baby weight."

I remove a cucumber slice from one eye and look her up and down. "Where are you keeping it?"

"My stomach jiggles now. I had twins. I gained forty pounds. Now I'm squishy in the middle."

"Might as well take you out back and shoot you."

Sadie giggles drunkenly.

I hear my kitchen door open. "Sebastian?" My little brother has arrived to raid the fridge and drink my liquor.

"In here!" I call. I hear his footsteps and I'm tempted to count to three, but I don't need to. He responds immediately with, "What the actual fuck?"

I can't see what he's seeing, because of the cucumbers on my eyes. But I can picture four people scattered around the rug with green goo on their faces. There's a mostly eaten pizza on the coffee table and beer cans lying about. Also, I'm pretty sure someone is playing an ocarina on Spotify.

"We're doing facials," Ash says from somewhere nearby. "But it might be time to rinse?"

"That sounds like a lot of work," Brynn mumbles from a corner. I agree. We all sigh in unison.

There's a pause, some ruffling, and then Bramly lies down on the floor and I hear him say, "I'm in."

Ash

This has been one of the strangest days in my life. I should probably turn in and just go to sleep, but I'm a little drunk, a lot relaxed, and the night has turned into a regular slumber party, with Bramly capturing everything in photos.

I don't know how that part got started, but sometime after our facials Bramly gets out his giant camera and starts snapping away. We're laughing at first, and then Sadie bursts into tears.

Too many beers, I think at first, but then she says in one long, impressive, operatic breath, "I don't like the way I look in pictures. Decker is right! I'm fat and squishy and I have cow boobs and lines where there shouldn't be lines and I found a gray pubic hair...a gray one! And once you go gray there's no hope and I need to leave my husband, but I don't want to die with my girls probably off to Europe or somewhere exotic like Cincinnati and

I'll be all alone, dying, in a studio apartment with nothing but canned peaches and gray pubic hair."

We all just process that for a minute, then Bramly says, "Sadie, you are one of the most beautiful women I've ever met and if I didn't prefer dick I would totally try to get you in bed."

"Really?" she asks, her voice tiny and hopeful.

He nods. "I would be all over you. In fact, come here." He takes her by the hand and leads her away.

They've been gone for at least fifteen minutes and I'm starting to wonder if Sadie might've convinced him to take her for a test ride, so Brynn, Braht and me sneak down the hallway to investigate.

I say *sneak*, but that's relative. Braht and I are quiet the only way drunks can be, which is really loud, but whispering. And Brynn, though perfectly sober, keeps talking about how her sea bands aren't fucking working and so she peels off to go puke.

Braht and I slink around the corner and see Sadie on that velvet couch, that same velvet couch where Braht took those amazing pictures. She's wearing only her bra and panties, and the look she's giving the camera, or maybe Bramly, is so sensual that I think I get pregnant just by looking at her.

She is *gorgeous*. I mean, she's beyond Earth Mother. She's a fucking goddess. And I get a little teary because this is the first time in a long while I've seen her smile and really own it that.

"Holy..." Braht says, and I feel a little twinge because I want him to have that reaction when he's looking at me. Against my better judgment I hear myself call out, "Me next!"

And Braht adds, "Then I get to be in the pictures with you."

I shush him to be quiet, but it's too late. Everyone has heard us. Even Brynn. And she's still in the bathroom making coughing noises.

"Isssookay. I'm a done here," Sadie says. "I think I should get dressed and drive home."

Before I can object, we hear Brynn call from the bathroom, "I'm driving you home!"

And just like that, they're packing up. Well, Brynn is. Sadie can only stare at herself in the mirror, going "blub blub" with her lips.

Bramly herds Braht and me toward the settee to take some photos. "This will be the first boudoir photo session for your eventual boudoir!"

I'm just about to ask what why he'd say that when I feel Braht behind me. His arms wrap around my hips and he pulls me close to his body. My ass is tucked in tightly against all that sleek skin and muscle. I can feel him hardening, so I smile a huge smile for the camera and make jazz hands. It's the drinks. And the stress.

"That's good," Bramly says, "but a little too Broadway. Smaller smile, Ash, and Braht, why don't you pull her hair off one shoulder. Yes! Like that. And now put your lips on her neck."

Warm, moist lips find my sensitive skin, and suddenly I have goosebumps. *Everywhere.*

"Yeah, that's hot." Bramly's voice sounds distant now. All my senses are focused on Braht's mouth, and Braht's hands, which are now slowly unbuttoning my shirt. I tip my head back, finding Braht's shoulder as his fingers glance past my tummy on their journey. It should feel weird that he's undressing me in front of a clicking camera. But my senses are too greedy for more touching to care.

He flicks my shirt away, and then his long fingers are on my skin. They tease the span between my hip bones, just over the waistline of my pants. A whimper escapes from my lips as Braht kisses my neck hungrily again.

The sound of the camera goes silent. All I can focus on is Braht's lips against my neck, the warmth of his breath, and his erection against my back. And I can't stand it anymore. I have to turn.

The moment I rotate in his arms, we're kissing. This is a kiss to end all kisses. This is a kiss that creates universes, or at least releases eggs in my uterus. This is a kiss that was made for birth control and I am one hundred percent into it.

He angles me around and leads me to the settee. And just as I'm lying down, feeling the velvet against my legs, because I'm apparently not wearing my pants anymore, he turns to Bramly and says, "Get. Out."

Then I forget Bramly and Brynn and Sadie because all I can focus on is Braht, and his very hard cock, and the way his hips move against mine. His kisses are full and deep. Each one is a blend of pressure, need, and power. We hear a door slam and the revving of cars and then everything is blessedly quiet, except for the beating of my heart.

"Ash," Braht says. I start to kiss him, but he stops me. I'm lounging on that goddamn wonderful settee, my legs open to him. I still have on underwear and my bra, but we could be done with those in seconds, so I start to unbutton his shirt. He stops me again by holding on to my hands. "Look at me," he says.

I do it because his tone commands me to. And then I shiver because I don't appreciate the fact that my body reacts just because a man orders me to.

"What?" I gasp. I'm so conflicted. The old Ash wants to let him hold me down right here and fuck me until I forget both our names.

But the new Ash knows better.

"Ash," he whispers, kissing me softly but still holding my wrists. He gives a little nudge with his hips and I can feel him under the fabric, just bursting to get free. I want him. God, how I want him. Inside me. *Now*. I groan a little because words are too hard to use.

He shakes his head. "I need to say this. I want you, you understand. All of you. Right now. But you need to know this. Outside of here, I will hold your purse. I'll get mani-pedis with you. I'll cry while watching Lifetime movies with you. I will hand over my man card and be your minion everywhere you want, except in the bedroom. In here, I want you to surrender, just a little bit, and let me take the lead."

I can't breathe. I really can't. I'm the one in charge. I'm always in charge. I make all the decisions. I plan things. I fucking orchestrate. He's asking too much.

"No," I say, and then take a deep breath. "That's not me." In fact, I need to get up. I can't lie on my back like this and just take it, even if it feels good. It's not who I am. I give him a shove and sit up.

He actually chuckles, like he heard every one of the traitorous thoughts I had a moment ago. One of his hands smooths my cheek. "Honey bear? I have to ask you a serious question."

"You can only ask it if you'll stop calling me honey bear."

"Did someone hurt you?"

Yes! Duh. It sounds like a ridiculous question until I realize he means sexually. "Not like that," I say quickly. "He messed with my head. But he wasn't violent."

"Mmm. Okay." He looks like he's deciding something. "Then let's compromise."

I'm immediately suspicious. Braht and I are too much alike for me to think that's a good idea. "Compromise" to me means I still win. "What did you have in mind?"

"I won't touch you. I won't hold you down like we both want." He winks. "This time you can still be the only one who moves."

"Okay." I like that plan fine.

"But..." Of course there's a *but*. There always is. "...But I get to tell you exactly what to do to me, and you have to do it."

Oh, fuck. On the one hand, I'll get to hear Braht's voice ordering me around. That makes me hot.

On the other hand, I'd have to obey him.

"Tough call," I say. "The power will go straight to your head."

"Maybe." He lies down on the settee, in the spot where I was just a second ago. Propping one knee up, he gives his shaft a slow stroke over his boxers. "All this could be yours."

My insides give a needy shimmy. "What would you tell me to do, anyway?" If he thinks I'm going to truss myself like a turkey and let him reenact Fifty Shades of Naïve, he's got another think coming.

"I'd tell you to fuck me," he says in a voice so low and husky that I want to rub the sound of it all over my body. "Why don't you just see how it goes?" He punctuates this idea with another slow stroke, and I notice the outline of his perfect cockhead straining against the cotton. I want that in my mouth. And wanting things makes me cranky. "Stop it."

He grins. "You've got it backward, honey. I give the orders." He drops his hand, though. And then he grips the waistband of his boxers and pushes them off. And I'm staring down at naked Braht on a velvet settee and there isn't enough willpower in the world to make me turn away from that.

"Don't swallow your tongue there, honeybunch." He tucks his hands behind his head. "First things first. Kneel down and kiss me."

That's easily done. I press a knee into the settee, lean over and kiss him right on the tip of his cock. I make it a nice wet one. With tongue. His clean, salty taste makes my face flush with desire.

"Ahhh!" he moans, and every gorgeous muscle in that six-pack gets tight. "Fuck, Ash. I meant on the lips."

"Shoulda said so, then," I giggle.

He laughs up at the ceiling. "You are such a handful. Get up here right now and give me your mouth. On mine," he adds quickly.

I guess I'm really doing this.

Slowly I maneuver until I'm right over him, and I watch as his greedy eyes take in the sight of my hair sliding over my bare shoulders. My movements are super slow, because I love the impatient look in his eyes. No lie—glaciers have moved faster than I do as I lean down toward his mouth.

When our lips touch, he groans.

I deepen the kiss, and he opens for me. Waiting. He doesn't jam his tongue in my mouth, but I think he wants to. I give him a few more light kisses before I can't wait anymore. And then I taste him, and he groans again.

I'm starting to catch on. Neither one of us has quite as much power right now as we wish we did. I can't do anything he hasn't asked for, and his hands are practically vibrating to reach for me.

He doesn't do it, though. He holds up his end of the bargain, and it's beautiful.

This is way, way more fun than all the gardening we did earlier today.

"Stop," he pants, and I withdraw my mouth immediately. "Now lose the panties."

I stand up and hook my fingers in the elastic. Then I push one side down my hip.

"Faster," he demands, his gaze like a laser on my body. "Drop them."

They hit the floor.

He's not done yet. "And the bra."

I unhook it slowly, as if the task requires great concentration. Meanwhile, he pants like an overheated St. Bernard.

When I'm finally naked, he gives me an evil grin. "Touch your tits. Cup them in your hands."

I slide my hands under my breasts and lift them. My breasts are heavy and full, the nipples super sensitive. Wowzers. I am seriously turned on. It's odd putting myself on display, but his voice makes me want to.

I swear his eyes roll back in his head. And his voice is thick with lust when he praises me. "That's more like it, honey bear."

"Hey!" It hardly sounds like a protest, though, because I'm teasing my nipples as I speak. "We had a deal. I am not your honey bear."

"Oh but you are. Touch your pussy now."

Uh oh.

I hesitate, and he smiles. "Spread your legs a little. I want to watch. Now use two fingers. Touch yourself."

Whew. Closing my eyes, I pass my fingers over my sensitive flesh just once. But I am embarrassingly wet for him. And when I open my eyes, he's grinning at me. "That's right. Now I want it. Bring those fingers here."

My knees threaten to buckle as he opens his mouth. *Holy moly.* Braht is a filthy boy. I'm impressed. I'm even a little intimidated. But I won't let it show. So I straighten my spine and pretend this is business as usual. No big deal. I'm just crossing the room like a badass to put two fingers into Braht's mouth so he can taste me.

He watches me approach with hungry eyes. And then his naughty lips clamp down over my fingers and his tongue laves over me, hot and determined. He gives an eager moan, and a suck, and my body temperatures shoots up another ten degrees.

That tongue. I want it all over me.

Braht releases my fingers on a sigh. His hips shift with desire. "Damn it, woman. Dying here." But his eyes are bright and happy, even if his dick is so stiff it looks painful. "Straddle me already."

I don't even hesitate. A moment later I toss a knee over him and sit up on his thighs. I reach for that impressive erection...

"Wait," he rasps. "Did I say you could touch it?"

My fingers hover over the prize while he watches me through lust-darkened eyes. "Don't disobey me, honey."

My everything quivers with need.

"Take my hand," he orders. I look at his hand where it's lying still on the velvet. "Go on. Pick it up."

I do this, and his skin is warm to the touch. I want this hand on my body.

"Use me to touch your breast."

I raise his palm to my body and we both sigh as skin meets skin.

"That's right," he says gently. "So soft. I could touch you all night long. I could fuck you all night long. Can't wait to be inside you."

My pussy clenches and he chuckles. I should hate this—letting him see how much I want it. And I should hate him for denying me. But I don't. I just close my eyes and sink into the sensation of his fingers on my tit. His thumb strokes over my nipple and goosebumps break out over my skin.

"My hand wants your pussy," he rasps. "Touch yourself with me."

All my hesitation is gone. I slide his long, smooth fingers down my body until the fingertips tickle my mound. He groans as I push his hand between my legs and then bear down, grinding shamelessly onto his palm.

"Yeah," he whispers. "Ride my hand. That's so fucking beautiful."

Let's just say that I agree. And that I'm shameless as I pleasure myself. I don't think about my swaying breasts or the way my hair is hanging down in sheets across my overheated skin. My pleasure builds, and I drop my hips a little lower, wanting more.

"You like?" he whispers. "I can't hear you. Let it out, honey."

I realize I've been holding my breath, and so I let it out in one big whimpering gasp.

"What was that?" he asks, tilting his head as if to hear me better. "I asked if you liked it. You have to answer."

"Yessss," I hiss. I can feel the edges of my senses drawing together. I'm reaching for it, and tuning him out.

"Stop," he says suddenly.

"What?"

"Listen, Ash. Stop moving."

That bossy voice penetrates my consciousness. Barely. But I bite my lip and stop. And that's when the first glimmer of humiliation arrives. My face heats. I don't look at him. I can't believe I've been shamelessly... Gah.

"Shh shh shh," he whispers. "It's only a temporary cease and desist. Grab a condom, sweetie."

Oh. That sounds like a terrific idea. Except, maybe we don't need one. "Do I have to?" I actually whine. "I mean...my birth control is bulletproof. And you're the most fastidious human I ever met, so unless there's a reason you need to be extra careful..."

He grins. "In that case, get on my dick. I want your tits in my hands, and I want you to lower yourself down on me and fuck me."

I have never obeyed an order so quickly in my life. Two seconds later I'm filling myself with him and attaching his hands to my breasts. Then I pause for a moment and look down into his gorgeous face.

"Wow," he says. "This is fantasy stuff right here. You're the sexiest thing on two long legs. And I can't get enough of you." His words aren't manipulative. They're simply grateful.

I'm in so much trouble here. I know this. But at the moment I don't have enough brain cells to worry about it. When I begin to move, he takes a deep, hungry breath. And then another. His ripped chest flexes beneath me.

"Touch me," he orders as I stare. And my hands are hungry for him. "That's my girl," he pants, and I light up with praise. "Now get down here and kiss me."

Yum. Another order followed without objection.

"Now say my name," he whispers against my lips.

I kiss him again, and then the word falls from my lips. "Sebastian," I whisper against his mouth, and I like the sound of it.

He moans, because he likes the sound of it, too.

I stop thinking then because I don't need to right now. All I need to do is be in this moment, with him, kissing and loving what he does to my body, how he plays me like a grand piano, how we're suddenly breathing and moving in unison. Nobody is in charge anymore. There's no ordering and no obeying. And there's no room for worry or even thoughts.

There's only room for what is.

Us.

16 DWEEB

Braht

I wake up to an empty bed and I panic. Seriously, I do. Ash is *gone*. I experience thirty seconds of intense displeasure before I realize...is that the scent of bacon floating toward me? And coffee? It is! Bacon and coffee!

Floating!

I get up and stumble into my boxers, following the scent, my semi-hard braht pointing the way, straight into the kitchen. And yes-there-is-a-Santa-Claus because Ash is there, wearing one of my dress shirts, buttoned only once, and she's naked underneath. I know it. I could just slide my hands up her legs and check, though. She turns to me, spatula in hand, and says, "I'm pretty sure I burned everything. I mean, I'm fairly certain eggs aren't supposed to have black parts on them, are they?"

To answer her, I just walk right up to her, wrap my arms around her and kiss her, bacon sizzling and coffee percolating around us. And yes. Burnt eggs. "Well, good morning," she says.

"Yes, it is."

It's a very good morning. I sorta want to high-five her and

dance around the kitchen to the tune of "We totally had amazing sex last night!"

But I do have my pride.

"Hand that over," I say instead. She hands off the spatula. "I've got this."

Burnt eggs slide into the disposal, and then I'm whipping up new ones. A three-minute omelet, bacon, coffee, and a naked-under-that-shirt Ash...what more could a man ask for?

I could ask for waking up like this every day for the rest of my life, but I'm pacing myself. I don't want to scare her off.

"How's your heart this morning?" I ask.

"Huh?"

"Your heart. Or, what's the reading on your anxiety meter? How you feeling?" I'm referring to the possible stalker camera. And, hey, it's okay with me if she also wants to admit that she's head over heels in love with me so we can elope to some warm Italian honeymoon where we'll shop for handmade shoes and eat pasta.

"I'm feeling..." She considers. I swear to God a sunbeam streams in from the window and highlights her flaxen hair. I've never used the word flaxen before, but it's the right word. She's fucking flaxen. And that semi-hard-on is now fully engaged. "I'm feeling good," she says. And then she smiles. This is the Ash I've been waiting for, the one that I saw glimpses of the first time I laid eyes on her. She's a piece of art.

And I am gone gone gone.

"Give me two more minutes," I say to focus on the omelet. She pours the coffee, grabs two plates and the bacon, and sits at the counter. In another minute, I've added in some goat cheese and chives to the eggs, turned them over so they're fluffy and beautiful, then I cut the omelet in half and slide it onto our plates.

"A girl could get used to this," she says.

"Okay," I say. She laughs, but I'm a hundred percent serious. "So, what's the plan?"

"The plan?" She takes a bite of the omelet and I just watch her reaction. It's melting in her mouth and a happy groan escapes her lips. "Ohmygod," she says. "You're amazing in bed and you can cook!"

"I also have good hygiene," the salesman in me adds.

She nods. "That you do. What do you mean by 'plan'?"

"Well, the creepy dude. Your ex? Dweeb or something?"

"Dwight," she says with a grimace. "I don't like to say his name."

"Hmm. I think you should. You're giving him power that way by staying scared of him. Name him. Say it. Dweeb. Dweeeeeeeeeeeeb."

A little laugh at that. "Okay. Dweeb."

"You can't live in fear of him, honey bear."

"I'm not your..." Her eyes widen as she remembers the fun we had last night. Then she blushes all the way down into the open collar of my shirt.

My dick does a happy dance in my boxers, and I have to change the subject or we're going to have to cook breakfast a third time because I'm going to push all the plates off the table and fuck her right here.

Whew.

Once I have myself back under control, I turn back to the important matter at hand. "Listen, we've got to figure out what he wants."

"What does it matter? I'm not letting him near me."

"I know, and I wouldn't let that happen. But getting rid of him will be easier if we can figure out why he's pestering you."

"Because he's a creep?" She cringes. "I testified against him. He's angry. Whatever he wants, it isn't good."

"Mmm," I say, unconvinced. I take a thoughtful sip of my coffee. The problem with Ash's logic is that men are simple creatures. We are goals-based thinkers. *Want beer. Find beer. Drink beer*, etc.

If that man is following Ash it's because he wants something concrete.

"He's been in prison for years, right? He probably has a probation officer he's eager to placate." Not for nothing have I been a TV addict my whole life. "Hounding you won't help his case. So I think there must be a reason he's doing it. Do you have any of his stuff?"

"God, no. I gave it all to the church sale. It was just clothes and classic rock CDs."

"You ended the marriage."

She nods. "I got an annulment. And—get this—I tried to sell the ring. He bankrupted me, too, when the feds seized our joint account. But the diamond he gave me? It was..." She blinks back tears. "It's really hard for a fashion addict like me to admit I was duped."

Oh, God. No! "A cubic zirconia?"

She nods, looking pained. "I was such a babe in the woods. It's embarrassing."

"You are still a babe," I point out. "A total babe." But I feel her pain. There's nothing wrong with a man buying the kind of ring he can afford. But to *pretend* he's giving her something valuable? "He wasn't a man, Ash. I can guarantee he coughed up his man card the first time he ever lied to you."

She puts her fork down on the plate. "Can we talk about someone else's stupidities, now? I threw the ring in the river and borrowed money from my parents instead. That's how I got my residential real estate license."

"Ah, parents. At least you've got a pair of those."

She looks sheepish. "Yeah. You're right. It could always be worse."

"You're not alone in this, okay? You've got me, and your besties. And Tom and even Bramly. Your parents. Heck, I'll bet you can even count on our little thriller writer. I bet she's fierce in a rumble. I can see her with nunchucks."

The smile returns to her face. "And a skintight bodysuit. I can see it, too. She could take out Dwi...*Dweeb*." Her smile gets stronger.

"That's the spirit. Now finish your coffee. We have a house to sell. And if you think of anything Dweeb might want from you, don't hold back, okay? He'll be easier to deter if we know what he thinks he can gain."

"Okay," she says softly. "Back to gardening, huh?"

"Nope," I say. "I'm calling in a landscaping company so we can work on our listing." And so that I don't turn into a grump monster in front of Ash again. "They'll have that yard under control by the end of the day. So dress appropriately for the office. But not too appropriately. We can reward ourselves with a quickie during lunch."

Her face takes on a dreamy expression, and I feel like I've won the fucking lottery.

17 I'M RIGHT HERE

Ash

When it's time to get ready for work, we realize there's a problem. When two people care equally about their appearance, not even a luxury-sized master bath is large enough.

There is a tussle over the shower. Braht wants at least a half hour in there to open his pores; I need the same amount of time to shave so I don't turn into a sasquatch.

We are forced to compromise; I get the shower, he sits on a fancy towel and practices his mindfulness techniques while the moisture in the air does its magic.

Then there's some playful and mutual groping, some teeth brushing, and a quickie against the wall.

Who knew Braht had such a thing for me in a pencil skirt and heels?

We take separate cars and routes to the office. And as soon as I step over the threshold of VanderMollen, there are no more thoughts of Braht touching me, or of nakedness in his bathroom. Nope. Not at all. I am the mistress of my domain and when I show up at work I am one hundred percent in The Fucking Emperor Of Selling Houses mode.

Emperor. Empress? Whatever. I'm the Emper.

A quick check of the whiteboard confirms my worst fears—whoever sells the mystery writer's house, me or Braht, will take the lead in securing the annual bonus. Even though I wrote a memo to management protesting this unfairness, they've still lumped all of Braht's current year production on the books for this branch.

For two seconds I consider cutting him off—withholding sex until I win the bonus.

However.

This snafu isn't actually Braht's fault. Moving branch offices wasn't even his idea. Besides, cutting him off would also harm me. Because goddamn it, he's a fucking sex god in pastel.

Since I took the circuitous route to the office (a girl needs her Starbucks), I've arrived a few minutes after Braht. Naturally I discover a pair of scissors spread eagle on my desk. And the stapler is performing...

This is getting out of hand.

Also, I've never been jealous of my scissors before.

Moving on. I replace those tools into their tidy places and don't even spare a glance in Braht's direction. It's fine if we're fucking like bunnies at his house, but the office doesn't need to know a thing about it.

The sound of office chair wheels rolling announces his presence a minute later. "Excuse me, platonic coworker. I have a question."

My eyes roll harder than Homer Simpson's bowling balls. "Yes, Guy Who Just Happens to Sit Near Me at the Office? How can I be of service?"

He grins, and my nipples harden. Damn it. Good thing I wore a sturdy bra. "When does the starting gun go off?"

"The starting gun?" I glance at his crotch and wonder how he can be so insatiable.

"For the house. When can I show Hill House? We need to

coordinate. The place is small inside, so if we double book, it won't work well."

"This is true. Wait—Hill House?" Isn't that the name of a horror story? I'm feeling a little too frisky to focus. Then I realize he's talking about our listing. "Hill House? Come on, the place is not that scary."

"Actually, it's literally Hill House. It's on Hodenpyl Hill. Anyway. How do you feel about a six p.m. official start time? We need to decide when we're ready for customers."

"Fine. Six. Your landscapers will be done, right? How much is this costing us?"

He gives a little shove off my desk and rolls back to his own. "Whatever the price, it's worth it. Got a call to make!"

Yikes. Then I guess I do, too. I need to find prospects before six o'clock. I take out my color-coded planner—the one where I keep leads—and flip through the pages, wondering who might want to see the place this evening.

I hear the chair rolling in my direction again a couple of minutes later. "Guess who has a showing at six p.m. to an owner of the Suck It Vacuum Company? Hmmm? Any guesses?" Braht asks.

"I give up," I say. "Who has a showing at six? Is it Dennie?" Dennie is another agent in our branch. There is a zero percent chance he has a showing, but I don't want to play Braht's reindeer games.

"Dennie?" Braht asks, like he's never heard the name before.

Meanwhile, ten feet away, Dennie is rotating his big, slow head trying to figure out who keeps saying his name. It's really no wonder I was the top saleswoman for two years before Braht showed up.

"It's not Dennie," Braht says. "I don't even know a Dennie. Dennie doesn't exist."

"I'm right here," Dennie says.

Braht continues. "It's *me*." Then he stands up and announces to the whole office in a Zeus-like voice: "I HAVE A SIX P.M.

APPOINTMENT TO SHOW HILL HOUSE AND I'M GOING TO TAKE ALL THE MARBLES!" Then he points to the whiteboard as if he's Babe Fucking Ruth calling his touchdown. Goal? Home run? Whatever. I don't follow sportsball.

"Okay, Spoiled Braht," I say. "Good luck with that."

There's a shocked silence in the office. Or maybe it's just a silence. Dennie is watching us, but there may be nobody home inside that cottage.

"What's that supposed to mean? Good luck?" Braht asks.

"It means good luck. How is that confusing?" I smirk when I say it.

"It's not *what* you're saying, it's *how* you're saying it." He leans in close to me and I can smell him. Not just how clean he is, but underneath that, pulsing, is the scent of man. Braht Man. I shake my head to clear it a little.

"I just said good luck. It means good luck. Now, get out of my office space." I say this forcefully and Braht gives me a look that says, *You're the boss now, but I'm the boss later*.

And I sigh because it's probably true.

"I don't like that guy," Dennie mutters from ten feet away.

I ignore him because that's what you do with Dennie.

Because I'm me, I do find a prospective buyer. And because I need that bonus and that new security system even more these days, I go the sneaky route.

Sometimes a girl just does what a girl has to do.

At five p.m. I tell Braht that I'm going out for drinks with the girls. Which is mostly true.

But first I drive over to Hill House for a secret showing. The clients are a newly married couple who are so bright and fresh and youthfully expressive that they are probably YouTube stars. Or maybe Snapchat. The way they're snapping pictures of everything, they must be Internet Famous, at least in their own minds. Every time I show them some unique aspect of the house (electric fireplace, granite countertops, old-school dumb waiter), one of them coos, "Just a sec!" and then they make a duck face and snap snap snap.

I may snap snap snap at any second.

This house is not large, but the showing takes forever. I try hard not to look impatient, but I want this house sold before Braht crosses the threshold. Unfortunately, these kids don't seem like they can make a decision about what kind of takeout to get, let alone whether or not to purchase a house.

"I love everything about it!" the girl says.

"Me too!" her hubby agrees.

"Indian or pizza?" she asks, while I break out in hives.

Young love is really annoying, all that hopefulness. She reminds me of myself when I took off with Dwight. Biggest regret of my life. I hope she has a separate bank account he doesn't know about.

"You know, it smells weird," she says all of a sudden. "Here, Lane, take my pic while I smell the air."

I try not to look, but he literally takes a picture of her with her nose slightly tilted like she's sniffing something that's not pleasant.

"Oh! I know what it is. It smells like my grandma!"

I can't tell if that's a good or a bad thing.

"Oh," hubby-Lane says.

"We could buy the house and demo it. Totally start from scratch," she says.

Uh oh. "Guys, this house would be tricky to scrape and rebuild. It's close to the waterfront, and the new rules about building near wetland areas would require an environmental review before you could build."

They both look at me like I've sprouted a second head which is speaking German.

"So we can't knock it down? Even though it's so small?" she asks.

"You might be able to. But if you design beyond the current footprint—which is grandfathered—your plans might not get board approval."

"Grandfathered?" Lane asks.

I sigh.

He smiles at his young wife. "You can take a picture of me with a big ol' hammer. Like I'm driving a ball peen hammer right into this wall here." Dumbass Lane smacks the walls and that's when I've had enough.

"Ball peen!" she giggles.

I look at my phone. "Oh, darn it!" I say. "Our time is up."

"But we're not finished!" Lane insists.

"We'll have to meet again," I say, knowing that it will never happen. They were never going to buy this place. I've been given the runaround again. I herd them toward their car, but it's slow going.

"Oh, I didn't get a shot of that creepy cat!" the young bride says. Before I can argue, she goes darting into the house. Lane follows her.

And that's when Braht drives up with his wealthy vacuum company-owning family. I'm so busted.

My nipples harden anyway.

Car doors slam, and I look down at my feet. A pair of Gucci loafers invades the patch of grass where my guilty gaze is focused. I cheated for nothing.

"Hello, Ash." Braht's voice is chilly.

"Hello, Braht."

"Funny. I didn't know you had a showing. You're supposed to put it in the schedule."

I say: "Um..."

From inside the house I hear, "Kitty kitty kitty!" And then the sound of a cat meowing unhappily. Actually, I'm pretty sure the cat is meowing cuss words.

Braht's clients are squinting up at the house. "May we go inside?"

"I was hoping the other client would come out first," Braht says through clenched teeth.

"We haven't got all night," the vacuum cleaner guy says. "I thought we were getting the very first showing?"

They all troop inside.

I wait.

Eventually my clients emerge, laughing about something or other. I say all the things I'm supposed to say, about how we'll be in touch.

We won't.

Unfortunately, Braht's clients emerge only two minutes later. "If you have anything larger," the wife says.

"Homes on the lake rarely come up," Braht says. "But you will be the first to know."

He and I stand side by side in silence while they drive away.

"We talked about this," he says when we can no longer see their car. "It's a small home, and we need to keep the showings from overlapping."

"I know," I whisper.

I need to apologize, but now another set of tires is coming down the gravel drive. Another car parks, and then he gets out, with another young couple in tow. "We were just in the neighborhood," Dennie says. "I know I didn't register for showing, but..."

"Go ahead," Braht and I say at exactly the same time.

"Jinx," we both say at the same time. Which is a double jinx.

Dammit. As if I need to be jinxed right now.

Dennie and his clients troop into the house behind us. I hope the cat has found a nice safe hiding place because this is turning into Grand Central Station.

"Look, I'm really sorry. I apologize for violating our plans. It wasn't the right thing to do, and I won't do it again."

"Oh, honey bear." He sighs. "I forgive you. We're in competition. There's no denying it. Besides, it makes me hot when you get feisty."

"I'm still sorry," I say, meaning it. "And I'll bet your next showing is a winner."

He grins. "It probably will be, because I'm wearing my lucky belt." There are alligators on it. Of course there are.

"I mean it," I say. "I hope it goes well." I remove a long blonde hair from his shoulder, smiling because it's mine. "I'm off to get drinks with the girls. Sadie's father hired a private investigator to prove that her husband is a cheat. She got the photos today, and she wants us there when she opens them."

He flinches. "Ugh."

"I know. But, listen. Do you think..." I clear my throat. "Do you think I could make it up to you later? After cocktails?"

"Hell yes," he says, eyeing me. "I'm available for makeup sex. Any day of the week. And now you can run along with your friends. I'll wait for Dennie to be done in there, and I'll lock up."

My eyes narrow. "Really?"

"Really."

"You don't have another showing, right?"

He smiles and shakes his head. "Nope. We're going to do everything on the books now. Should we pinky swear?"

I offer him my pinky and we shake.

Then he grabs me for a big, hungry kiss. With lots of tongue.

My nipples are like bullets by the time I have to drive away.

18 WINE BAR AND SADNESS

Ash

"I need a selfie," I tell my friends. It occurs to me that I'm acting like the couple I showed Hill House to, but I'm not doing the whole duck-face thing, so this is really okay.

We're at the bar again. It's a wine bar with sophisticated cheeses so we feel dignified. And Brynn pretty much just craves cheese right now. Sadie can only stay a half hour because her girls are at a coworker's house to develop socialization skills AKA a playdate, and she doesn't want to impose too long. "Okay," Sadie agrees, moving into the shot.

We all smile and—per tradition—I take the photo because I have the longest arms. "Sloth arms," Sadie once called them.

"Cool. Thanks." They take their seats as I quickly text the photo to Braht, to prove that I made it safely here.

I still feel like a jerk for showing the house on the sly, but if I don't keep my annual sales bonus, I can't afford the security system. Which I need. Because sooner or later Braht will get tired of me staying with him. He is a man, after all. His dick will start pointing at some other woman and I will have to move on. I know this from experience.

A moment later my phone pings back. Braht has sent me a picture of his, erm, package. Looks like he's at his house hanging out in a silk kimono and nothing else. I'm suddenly very hungry for bratwurst.

Then I tell myself to focus, because I need to be present, mentally present for my friends. This isn't just a fun meet-up. We're here to help Sadie—to be her soft place to land, if she starts to fall, and everything in my gut says she's going to.

"Well?" I ask.

"Man, I wish I could drink," Brynn says.

"I'll maybe drink enough for you," Sadie says. "Once my kiddos are asleep." We watch in horror-movie anticipation while Sadie pulls an envelope out of her bag. The private investigator her dad hired has hit paydirt, and it's time to review the evidence.

"Are you sure we should be seeing these?" Brynn asks, slurping her soda.

"Oh, I'm positive," Sadie says through gritted teeth. "I mean, I'm not going to post them on the internet. I'm not going to ruin my husband's career. But the PI said it's pretty definitive. So let's get this over with."

The first glossy photo shows her husband Decker waving to someone.

In the next shot, a young woman approaches him on the street. "Hey," Brynn says. "They're outside Hop Cat! I puked in those bushes just last week!" She sounds kind of proud.

"Well, hold on to your cookies. I'm sure it gets worse." Sadie shows us the next photo, of Decker and the girl greeting each other with a kiss in the next shot.

We all fall silent. I wouldn't have guessed that this would be so hard to look at. He's not my husband. But the sight of her hand resting so casually on his camel overcoat makes me want to scream.

Flip. Sadie shows us a photo where they're seated at a table.

Flip. They're getting into her car.

Flip. They check into the H&I hotel. It used to be the Holiday Inn but was purchased by a new company who apparently wanted to save on signage.

Flip. He's got her on her hands and knees. It's a perfect shot of Decker's bare ass as he...

"I think I'm gonna..." Brynn runs for the ladies' room.

Sadie puts the photos away and takes a sip of wine. "Now all that's left is to confront him." She sounds remarkably steady. Reserved or resigned, I'm not sure.

"You want me there with you when you tell him?" I offer. "I don't mind. I know some karate and I want to see Dick-her's face when he sees he's been found out."

"Dick-her!" Sadie smiles for the first time tonight.

Gallows humor. It's been our friend for a long time, now.

Brynn returns, and Sadie parks her cheek in her hand. "I'm ready to divorce him. My father and I are going to confront him together tomorrow night when he gets home from his business trip. By then, my sister and I will have already packed up his things and put them in a U-Haul. I'm handing him the key. That's it. Evicted."

"You are fierce," I say. "I'm in awe."

Sadie shrugs. "Still. I really need to understand, if only for professional purposes. How do we end up with these assholes? All three of us. Brynn had Steve you had Dwight. And I had Dick-her."

We laugh, because Dick-her is still funny.

"Tell me. I need to know."

"Oh, it's easy," Brynn says with a wave of one hand. "In my case, it was insecurity. I was the slightly overweight, slightly under-tall girl. Steve was the first guy who came along to say he was interested for the long haul. And even if his interest actually lasted about ten minutes, I clung on. There were warning signs everywhere and I ignored them."

"Like what?" I demand. Because I've already proven that my

147

judgment is even worse than hers. I'm the only one sitting here whose ex did seven years in jail.

Now I start to wonder if I'm ignoring all the red flags Braht is waving. His flags are probably pastel. But still. What if he's too good to be true? "Girls, what *are* the warning signs? We need to codify these. For science. Like, we need a formula we can plug in the variables, and arrive at an answer. Will the guy turn into an asshole? Or not."

Sadie lifts her face. "Solve for D, where D equals the chances that a man is revealed to be a douchenozzle."

We all fall silent for a moment, thinking about the inputs to this equation.

"For me, the warning sign I missed was the cable guy," Brynn says suddenly.

"The what?"

"I just thought of this recently," she says, folding her hands. "Right after Steve and I moved in together, we had the cable installed. The guy messed it up, and Steve blew a gasket." She smiles, because unlike Sadie and me, this is in her past.

"Well," she continues. "Fast-forward several years, and Tom and I order the premium package—ultra-lightning-fast cable Wi-Fi for the new cottage. They've sent out the guy three times now, and it still isn't quite right. We're still waiting for one more part to arrive. But Tom has been a prince about it at every visit. He says, 'that poor slob has the same low-wage job that I almost ended up with if I hadn't gotten my first network gig.'"

That does sound like something Tom would say. But Tom is the perfect man.

"Wow. His empathy runs deep," Sadie says.

"Yeah," Brynn sighs.

"Dick-her would have ripped the cable guy a new one. I think Brynn is onto something. We can't trust what they say to *us* when they want to get in our pants. And there are other caveats. One thing that impressed me about Dick-her in the early days was that he's nice to his feeble granny."

"Is feeble granny loaded?" I ask. My bullshit meter is very finely tuned these days.

"Yup!" Sadie says cheerfully. "Honest to God, they should take away my therapist's license. Who needs a therapist who can't see all these red flags?"

"Hey! That's not fair," I insist. "Because you're not having sex with your clients' families. It's sex that confuses everything. You couldn't see Dick-her's flaws because you saw his dick instead. You used to tell us that the sex was really good. When there are pheromones in the air, it makes everything cloudy like fog on your glasses. But better."

"Steve never made me tingle," Brynn argues.

"Right. And that's why your breakup was less of a shock. She who does not tingle has the presence of mind to end things herself."

Sadie smiles at me. "Then *you* must be our most avid tingler. I didn't notice he was sexing up the nanny. But you didn't see illegal activity and embezzlement."

"Well..." *Cough.* She has a point.

"Ha! That does explain a lot," Sadie says.

"We never liked him," Brynn adds sadly.

"I know, okay! This formula needs a sex variable. The better the sex, the more you're willing to ignore."

Which means that I can't possibly see Braht's flaws. He's already erased part of my brain with his dick.

I behaved just the same way with Dwight, who was really attentive in bed. I rushed our relationship. I didn't listen to my friends. On some level I knew eloping in Vegas was dumb. Part of me knew he'd suggested it to avoid my family's scrutiny.

"I knew he wasn't a great person," I admit. "He would have tried to sleaze the cable guy out of some extra equipment. *You don't really need those wrenches, right?*"

My friends laugh. "So how good *was* the sex?" Sadie wants to know. "I'm picturing a nine-inch penis that vibrates on several different settings."

"Not nine inches at all. His dick was like him: short and stocky. And it didn't have any mechanical advantages," I say slowly. Dwight was a handsome guy, but he wasn't extraordinary. Ever since our horrible breakup I've been wondering why it was so easy for him to keep me under his spell. "Dwight was more about...enthusiasm over technique or equipment. He was so damned confident. Always in charge. My job was just to go along with it, and I was perfectly fine with that. I gave him everything he ever asked for: my coochie, my self-esteem. My bank account number."

And then my job. Dwight had actually stolen from the commercial real estate development firm where I worked. Which was how I ended up unemployed.

The only saving grace of his demise was that his overconfidence led him to take foolish risks. He signed checks with my name, but when they were examined, the signatures weren't even close. Over the course of forty-eight very bad hours I was interrogated and then quickly released.

He was so certain of getting away with everything that he didn't bother doing a good job covering his tracks.

"Oh honey," Brynn says. "Those weren't great years. But you are a badass for putting him in jail and then getting on with your life."

"I thought I was," I say slowly. "But now that he's out, I'm not quite so sure I really did that. I'm still dragging them around with me, damn him!"

"If it's any comfort, you're not alone," Sadie says. "Half of my practice is people still trying to distance themselves from horrible people in their pasts." She frowns. "No, not 50%. It's more like 90%."

"Who does that leave?" Brynn asks.

"The woman who thinks the squirrels run the country with her long-dead twin brother. And another guy who thinks his toaster is watching him."

"See, Ash? It could always be worse," Brynn says.

I nod because it could be. Sadie puts her head on the table. Brynn reaches for her hand and I rub her back. We just sit like that for a moment. This shit is hard, but at least we're in it together.

19 REALLY GOOD GIN

Braht

Earlier, when I pulled up to Hill House and saw Ash, my first reaction was, "What the hell?" But my second reaction was "Hell yes!"

I love it when she one-ups me. She gets all fiery. For a while there, I was worried that this Dwight/Dweeb situation was going to extinguish that light in her for good, but he hasn't. And he won't. Not if I have anything to say about it.

So I'm actually glad she's out with her friends tonight. Everyone deserves to hang out with their besties. I've got Tom when I need him and Bramly is always in the background.

I'm lounging at home when Ash texts me a picture of her and Sadie and Brynn. They look shiny and happy. So I text Ash a picture of me, in bed, wearing silk. All artists make difficult choices so I opt to crop out the gin and tonic and the crackling fire in favor of a close-up of my crotch.

That's artistic, too.

I'm thinking luxurious, horny thoughts when I spy something out the window. It's a tiny red light out there in the darkness.

The kind you see on a camera.

For a moment I don't really react. I take another sip of my gin and tonic (it's Plymouth gin, my favorite. Because cheap gin is a crime). I glance around the room, wondering if something in here could cause a reflection.

But no. Nothing of mine should be shining on the window. And anyway, I know what I'm seeing. There's someone outside my bedroom window.

My heart rate doubles, but I set the drink carefully down on my nightstand (quarter sawn oak. A Stickley reproduction.) Then I ease myself out of bed and walk calmly to the door of my room.

Jumping out of the window won't work this time, because I'm on the second floor. So I dart down my stairs, slide on my Guccis and exit hastily through the front door. As soon as I'm outside, I can hear him.

Footsteps running away, toward the back of my property.

Shit.

I give chase, but when I round the corner of the house, he's already out of sight. So I reverse course, walking out to the quiet street instead. I live in a neighborhood with three- and four-stall garages. So unless someone's having a party, there are rarely cars parked on the street.

And yet there's an aging '72 El Camino muscle car, the kind of car that's like a mullet: business in the front, party in the back, parked three houses away.

I trot right over there, memorizing the license plate number on my way. I keep my head up because I don't need this asshole surprising me in the dark. The streetlamp gives me just enough light to make out a camera case on the back seat.

Shit.

I stand there and look around for a while, waiting. That fucker is probably somewhere in the shadows watching me. And I've left my own house unattended.

So the only thing to do is go home and lock the door. Which I do. But then I get out my computer and Google private detectives.

Ash might not like me meddling. But she gave me the idea in the first place when she mentioned her friend Sadie.

I can't sit here and do nothing. If I call the cops with a vague report that someone pointed a camera into my bedroom, there won't be a thing they can do. They're going to assume I'm paranoid.

A PI will care, though, because I'll pay him to care.

The first guy I dial picks up on the first ring, too. "This is Hank Miller. How can I help you?" His voice sounds like life has kicked him around a bit, and then he turned around and sucker-punched life out. He scares me a little.

He's perfect.

"Hi, Hank. I need to know if my girlfriend's jackass of an ex-con ex-husband is stalking us, and why. I'm going to give you a name and a license plate number, for starters."

There's a pause. "This case isn't about cheating?"

"Nope. Why?"

"They're all about cheating. I get so tired of shooting pics of guys' bare butts."

Huh. "This case does not involve any bare butts," I assure him. "But if it's all the same to you, let's get this license plate down on paper. I have some very good gin to drink."

"I hear that," he says and I can actually hear the ice clink in his glass.

An hour later I hear my garage door open. And a minute after that, Ash enters the kitchen looking disheartened. "Whatcha drinking?" she asks. "Actually, I don't care what it is. But make mine a double." She tosses her coat onto a stool and heads for the living room, then sits down heavily on the sofa.

"Rough night?" I ask while double-checking my home security system. And I've already shut all the drapes in the house. I can't decide whether or not to spill my guts about spotting that camera outside. I'll tell her everything I know, of course. It's just that I won't know more until the PI gets a chance to do his thing.

"The roughest. Poor Sadie."

I sit down next to her and she puts her head on my shoulder. "Men are such assholes," I say.

She chuckles. "You don't have to be a traitor to your people."

"Well. Men make up at least half the assholes on the planet. So it's true no matter what." I know quite a few of them, too. My father, for starters.

Ash doesn't comment. She only snuggles closer.

I pull her into my arms and sigh. We're both a little down. Obviously. That explains why we're not tearing each other's clothes off, and why my dick is, well, down.

I take a breath of her fruity scent and realize that this is nice, too. Very nice.

"Braht?"

"Hmm?" And, *whoops*. Spoke too soon. I chub up just from hearing her say my name in that breathy voice.

"My parents have invited us to the cottage for a couple of days."

Oh. "When?"

"Tomorrow night. Mom says she wants us to spend time there once more before they close it down for the season. I'm on the fence. I should be showing the heck out of Hill House, but it would be good to get away. I could make excuses for you and go alone."

"I'll go," I hear myself say.

She lifts her face to look at me. "Really? Because you could also sell the listing out from under me while I'm gone. I probably deserve it."

"You probably do." I put a finger on her nose. "But I'm not sure it matters. Dennie's showing went really well. That young couple wants to tear it down."

"That's so tricky," she protests.

"It is, unless you're two married architects who can design a showy new home on the old one's exact footprint."

Her eyes widen. "Oh. Shit."

"Yeah. I think we'll have an offer by morning."

She puts her head down on my shoulder again. "Fucking Dennie. He couldn't sell an oasis to thirsty nomads."

"Life is unfair. On the other hand, this means we can go have more cottage sex." I give her a squeeze. "I have fond memories of that little bed."

"You'll have to go there as Hunter again," she says to my neck. "That's weird."

Oh, Ash. You have no idea. "Wouldn't you know? I'm already used to it."

20 WEINER AND BALLS

Ash

I think I'm depressed. It's got nothing to do with Dennie selling our listing. It's actually cute to see him walking around the office all puffed up like a peacock. "Guess who sold a house? Me! This guy right here! In your face, Braht!"

I honestly think it's the first house he's ever sold. Mostly he's just in the office to notarize things and pick up Starbucks. So, good for him.

What's depressing is that Dennie's sale leaves Braht and me neck and neck on the leaderboard. Nothing is decided, and I'm still on edge.

Damn Braht.

I'm also a little jealous of the couple who are buying Hill House. That will cost a wad. Must be nice to have so much money that you can buy a house for a fortune, tear it down, and then spend another fortune rebuilding. All I do is worry about money, and I can't tell my parents because then they'll try to help.

The clock is ticking on year end, too. Even if I got a new listing right this minute, it might not close in time to count. But I won't give up yet. I'm not a greedy girl. But I have needs. All I want is enough money for my home, some quality appetizers at happy hour, and a security system.

Okay. And a day at the spa. I really feel like I've earned that after powering through all my Dwight-induced stress.

One surprising bright light in all of this murkiness is the cottage trip with Braht. No—Hunter. It will feel ridiculous to spend another night calling him by the wrong name.

I wish I'd been honest from the start and just told my parents the truth. I had a million chances to come clean, but I stuck with the delusion. Obviously I'm good at those.

And then Braht slipped so seamlessly into the role that it stunned me. When my parents call him Hunter he turns immediately at the sound of that name. It's kind of freaky what a good actor he is.

Braht is pretty much good at everything.

And I mean everything.

I'm worried I might be falling for the fashionable fucker.

Fuck.

It's November, and the highway scenery is just breathtaking. The trees are almost bare of color, but what's left is stunning: bright yellows, reds, a lick of piney green. It's like the forest sets itself on fire for a couple of weeks and then rises from the ashes in the spring.

I should do that, too. Okay—I don't actually want to set myself on fire. But somehow I will rise from the ashes of this shitty situation and emerge stronger on the other side.

What stickers would work for this? A phoenix, maybe. And do they make washi tape with tiny little ass-kickings depicted on it?

"You are deep in thought," Braht remarks. He reaches across the car and puts his hand on my thigh. Literally *right* on my thigh because I'm wearing boots, a skirt, tall, cable-knit socks and a cashmere sweater.

And now that warm hand is starting to slide northward, under the hem of my skirt, and slowly dancing over to the seam of my panties.

"Braht..." I warn, a little breathily. I'm actually driving, so it isn't safe to turn me on right now.

"What? You just seem really serious and you scare me when you're serious so I thought I'd lighten the mood."

His finger ventures further, that fucker. He lightly circles my clit, and the only thing protecting me from instant orgasm is a thin layer of cotton and about ninety seconds. "Stop!" I say, but laughing. "I am not getting into a car accident."

"At least you're wearing nice underwear. So if the ambulance comes, they'll say, 'wow, she's wearing nice underwear. She must be a good girl. Not the kind who pulls over to let a guy fuck her in the back seat.'"

"None of that," I say. Sadly, his fingers retreat. I miss them already. "Later you can have your filthy way with me."

He smiles at that and we drive up the steep hill and park.

When we get to the door, though, a sense of doom lands swiftly on my shoulders like a lead blanket. "What's wrong?" Braht asks.

I take a deep breath, just to confirm. "Oh god, Braht..."

"Hunter," he reminds me.

"Hunter..." I turn to him and in a stage whisper I say: "Take a whiff."

He does. "Ehm?" He looks really confused. "What *is* that? Did the sewer back up?"

I shake my head. "It's worse. That's my mother's cooking."

Braht

I am a strong man. I really am. But this is going to be a test of my fake boyfriend skills. I sort of thought Ash was joking last month when she told me that only her father could cook. I mean, that apple pie her mom made was amazing, so I thought maybe Stuart was just giving Beth a break by doing all the other cooking.

Now I understand the enormous error I've made.

"Soup's on!" Beth says. Stuart is in the living room and we suddenly hear Frank Sinatra singing to us in surround sound. Everything is lovely so long as you've lost your sense of smell. I grab hold of Ash's hand because she's actually shivering.

"So, Ma," she says. "Why did you cook tonight?"

Beth doesn't answer right away. There's some banging, an "ouch," and a puff of smoke. She's forbidden us to help, so we're both sort of watching in polite horror.

Stuart comes in and sits down. "I just wasn't in the mood," he says. My Spidey sense is telling me that something is going on in the Power household. My Spidey sense also tells me to be quiet and ride it out. Ash squeezes my leg and confirms my instinct.

"Here you go," Beth says proudly. "Guests first!" and she hands me a plate. I just...I can't...and I have to hold in a giggle. I really do. Grown men cry and grown men giggle and this is worth a giggle for sure, because there are two boiled potatoes on my plate and a terrifyingly long...what the fuck is that?

"Kielbasa!" Beth says. "I took a class and we made our own! Handling that meat was a little troublesome, but Chef Rinaldo says I did a great job."

I set the plate down in front of me. And just blink. It's a long, reddish-purplish kielbasa with two white potato balls at the bottom. I swear to god, we're having dick for dinner.

I look to Ash and gulp. She's smiling at me. "Try some sauerkraut with it," she says, then whispers, "You'll need it." And then she thunks down an enormous spoonful of the stuff on my plate.

I wait for everyone to sit down at the table before taking a tentative, dainty bite. And it crunches. The kielbasa crunches! A sausage should not crunch. I look back to Ash in horror and she nods and takes a very long sip of water.

This is a crossroads. The choices are bleak. Either I offend Beth by passing up her cooking. Or I offend my digestive system by remaining the perfect boyfriend so that Ash will eventually understand that I really am here for her.

Panic grips me, because it's a difficult choice. I need Ash. I value her. Yet I also value my intestines.

But then I do a little more cost-benefit analysis and realize I can relax. The path is clear. Some temporary discomfort would be worth a lifetime of Ash. So I will eat this meal. And smile. And love it. Every single horrible bite.

What's that saying? You know how you eat a whale? One bite at a time.

Yet I'm only on bite number two. It's going to be a long dinner.

Somehow I manage. God help me, I do. We make small talk and that's lovely and all, and I just keep taking bite after bite. Ash looks at me sort of impressed at first and then leans in when her mom isn't looking and says, "What are you doing? You're trying to kill yourself!" I just smile and take one last long, dry swallow of that weiner on my plate. Maybe it's not kielbasa at all. Maybe it as an actual cow's weiner. My stomach is starting to rumble.

I really need some fresh air. Like, right now. Luckily, my phone is vibrating in my pocket. A quick look reveals that it's the PI calling, so I actually have a wonderful excuse to step outside.

"Beth, Stuart, if you'll excuse me. I hate to be rude, but this is a call I've been expecting."

"Do you have a lead on selling a house?" Ash asks me, and in a tone that is clear she means you-better-not. I just shrug my shoulders like, "I dunno," and then step out into the brisk November air.

My stomach rumbles fiercely when I stand up, but I grit my teeth and lurch toward freedom.

"Hello?" I answer the call the second I step outside.

Hank doesn't bother with small talk. Hank is all business. I love Hank. "Listen, I found the guy and I put a GPS tracker on his car. You can access it by clicking on the link I sent you."

"What link?"

"In the text message I sent you. I've sent you about ten. The dude was near your girlfriend's house, so I thought you'd want to know. If you got any questions, call me." And then he hangs up.

He's not rude or anything, he's just gruff. Maybe his favorite sportsball team is on TV.

I take a quick look at my text messages and sure enough. There they are:

Perpetrator's legal name is DWIGHT RICHARD ENGERSOLL. The El Camino is registered in his name.

Perp has long list of violations. Mostly white-collar crime, but also prison violence.

This is not a guy to be messed with. I don't like the smell of him. He stinks of desperation.

For Hank's sake, I'm hoping that's a metaphor.

Talked to force friend. They've got an APB on him. Missed parole hearing.

That last text is the only good news. If Dweeb went back to jail for jumping parole, that would make Ash's life easier. But he was near Ash's house?

I'm starting to feel a little kielbasa green.

And then I follow the link to his tracking app, and I feel downright nauseated. A map fills the screen of my phone. Dwight's tracker is a red dot on a street. A very familiar street. Right this second, Dwight is parked around the corner from my house. My. House.

Holy shit. If I were less of a man, I might pee myself right now.

Okay. Now is not the time to panic. Now is the time to make a plan.

Except I'm experiencing a rare caveman moment. I want to jump in my car and go find that fucker. I want to attack him in his

El Camino. I want to take the law—and his throat—into my own hands.

Smart Braht wouldn't do that. He'd stay calm, enter the house and discuss this with Ash and her parents. And maybe call the police. This is the point where that would make good, logical sense.

But there is no Smart Braht right now. Smart Braht has left the building. Smart Braht took off when he decided to impress the love of his life by eating the worst dinner on the planet.

In Smart Braht's place is very angry Hunter. I'm Hulk Hunter. Instead of talking to the Powers, I take a quick peek in at them. They seem to be having an intense conversation, and Ash looks upset.

Shit.

Even Hulk Hunter doesn't like it when Ash gets stressy. So I take a seat on the porch and do some alternate nostril breathing and meditate. I can do this. I need to stay calm for my girl. She needs me.

Ash

It happens when I'm watching Braht dry-swallow my mom's heinous homemade kielbasa. I realize something. I'm actually falling in love with him.

And this is very, very bad.

I can't fall in love with Braht. I can't fall in love with *anyone*. Ever again. I trusted Dwight, and look how that turned out. Sadie trusted Decker, and now she's going to be a single mom to twins while he runs off to boink a twenty-year-old nanny who is captain of her cheerleading team.

Brynn trusted...Brynn never trusted Steve. They were just bored and decided to get married. But she trusts Tom and Tom... has so far turned out to be amazing.

I'm very, very confused.

I take a nice long sip of water to kind of clear the lump in my throat. The lump is half emotion, half bad kielbasa. Even my lump is confused.

At first I hated Braht. It was fun hating him. He was a great nemesis, all cocksure and dressed in 1980s colors. He's still a great nemesis. He's also something more.

Dinner is long and a bit awkward. And not just because of the wretched food. Mom and Dad are being kind, but there's something they want to talk to me about. The first sign was that Mom cooked at all. The only time Dad lets her in the kitchen is if he's had a colonoscopy and/or dental work. And he hasn't had either of those today, I'm pretty sure.

I can also tell that whatever they want to talk to me about, it's bad. Really bad. I lose whatever appetite I had, push the plate away from me, and just sit back and watch Braht take one valiant, brave bite after another.

Yep. Totally falling for him.

I hear his phone buzzing long before he acknowledges it. I give him a nod so he knows it's okay and he steps out. Hopefully he'll take a little walk or something so that my parents have enough time to tell me whatever they want to tell me.

Braht shuts the door behind him and it's not a second later that Dad says, "Honey, we've got to tell you something." Every muscle in my body clenches as Mom reaches for his hand. Holy shit. My eyes get all teary because I know they're going to tell me that one of them is dying.

Can we just go back and start today over and have everything be golden and wonderful? Actually, can we go back a little further and make sure my mom misses that chef class for fresh weiner making, because what the fuck was she thinking?

"Honey, you okay?" My dad again. I remember to breathe.

"It's better if we just tell her, Stu."

He nods. I'm going to pass out. *Please don't be dying don't be dying don't be...* "We're putting the cottage up for sale."

It's like there was this giant universe-size vacuum that sucked all the air out of the room and now pushes it all back in. "Is that it?" I cry. "Thank God! I thought one of you was dying."

Dad laughs. "Dying? What? No. We're healthy as can be. In fact..."

"We're moving to Canada," Mom finishes.

Cue the air suckage again. I can't process this. Any of it.

"Why?" is all I can manage.

"Well," Dad says, "We had different plans for our retirement but you remember..."

"Your retirement fund," I supply. They lost it all when their investment management company—HIMCO—turned out to be a Ponzi scheme.

"Right," Mom says gently.

I was sixteen years old when they learned that my father's inheritance and every dollar they'd ever saved had vanished into the mist. It wasn't just us, though. Lots of people in West Michigan were caught up in it.

That was a scary time. We moved into a crappy apartment so both Mom and Dad could stop paying our big fat mortgage. When you're sixteen and your clothing allowance gets cut to nothing, it feels like the world is ending.

At the time I thought money troubles were the worst thing in the world. But then I married an asshole and learned that there are worse things.

Moving on.

"We had hoped that we could always keep this place," Dad is saying. He pats the dining table lovingly. "There's no mortgage on the cottage, so we held on. It was our last real investment, and thank God, right?"

I've heard this before, so I just nod.

"But I'll be seventy next year, and I want to retire. We've been saving as much as we can, but in order to retire I need to sell the cottage."

"I understand," I choke out. But I'm sad. There've been nineteen years since the collapse of HIMCO. I thought that maybe it was enough time to restock the coffers. But now I realize that was just wishful thinking. My parents don't share the details of their finances with me. I shouldn't have assumed that everything was fine.

"It would have been nice to keep it in the family forever," my dad says. He's in pain. I can hear it in his voice. "We always pictured winterizing the place and spending time here with you, and your husband and kids..."

Awkward, awkward silence.

"This is all my fault," I blurt.

"No!" Mom takes over. "Life doesn't always turn out the way you plan. We can see how independent and successful you are. And maybe you'll get that husband and kids someday, especially with Hunter in the picture..."

But that isn't what I meant at all. They have to sell the cottage, and it's partly because of *me*. Five years ago, when my life fell apart, they were there for me. Dwight went to jail and I was jobless. They paid for my real estate licensing course and they put off replacing their old car. Because of me.

I'm a spoiled brat. I really am. I never paid back that money. I thought everything was on a permanent upswing.

And now this.

"...But the renovation would require a capital infusion that we just don't have," my father says. "I've done the math a hundred times. If I sell the house in town, there still just isn't enough capital to fix this place up. Instead, there's a small place up in Ottawa that's available. It's near where I grew up. I've lived in the U.S. for your whole life, but it would be really cost-effective to retire there." Dad's eyes are teary too and his voice is thick. Mom takes over.

"We so wanted to be able to leave this place to you someday. Keep it in the family. But we just can't afford it. If we sell it, we can get that nice place up in Ottawa and you can visit anytime you want."

Dad and Mom both reach for my hands and it's like we're

about to have a séance, but there's no spirit to call in and rescue us now. "We're so sorry we've let you down," Dad says.

Let me down? Let *me down?* "You haven't let me down!" I bellow. "You've loved me. You've supported me. You've shown me what a healthy relationship looks like. I love you both so much and I am going to help you."

"I thought you could," my mother says gently. "You and Hunter could work together on it and we'll get the best price we can."

"The listing will be mine alone," I say quickly. Because old habits die hard. "But I will do everything I can," I say. And I'm suddenly feeling sniffly. Then we're all crying. It's really like a Christmas morning coffee commercial. Cue the tissue box.

I hug them both, blow my nose and then say, just because I really need to be honest with my parents, "Please promise me you will never make kielbasa again."

Mom laughs and nods.

Dad says, "Thank heavens!"

I smile, but inside, I am breaking a little. I love this place. I don't want to give it up. I think maybe there might be a way to save it. Possibly. If I'm very, *very* lucky. But I can't talk about it yet, because it might not work. I'll need some quality time alone with my calculator and my best pens and some motivational stickers to figure it out.

And even then the math just might not work out.

That's life, I guess. It kicks you when you're down. Life kicked my family down and it's just never let us get back up.

That's when Braht pushes open the door and gives me a tender smile.

So I burst into tears again.

21 BIG PLANS AND LITTLE EPIPHANIES

Braht

It shouldn't feel this good to hold someone who's sad. I wish Ash weren't distraught right now. I'd do anything to make it better. But the way she throws herself into my arms gives me so much hope. Right now, she's chosen me to be her rock. And I will never let her down.

"I'm sorry," she mumbles into my shirt collar.

"Shh," I say, running a hand down her hair. "It's all right." Whatever she's crying about right now, I will fight it with my bare hands. I will rip its throat out with my teeth and destroy it with fire.

"Get some sleep, sweetie," her mother urges. "Everything looks a little bleak right now, but it will really be okay."

"I kn-know," Ash stammers. "It's just a house. Nobody died." She takes a deep breath. She says good night to her parents and then she lets me steer her up to our little love shack. I actually get hard as we climb the stairs. The night we spent together here was one of the best nights of my life.

But poor Ash isn't thinking sexy thoughts right now. She's

running a hand slowly up the carved bannister, taking in the details of this cottage as if she'll never see it again.

I think I can guess that this house is somehow doomed. I feel a little sad about it too, and I don't even have the full story. But there ought to be a shrine on this property—like those historic battle markers you see for Civil War sites.

On October tenth on this spot Sebastian Braht first seduced the woman of his dreams. Casualties: none. Weaponry: dirty talk and first-class salesmanship. Result: only one party shot his cannon, but both parties declared victory multiple times.

Ash gets ready for bed in a daze. She's wearing that same threadbare, boobalicious T-shirt again, and I can't wait to lick her everywhere. As soon as I figure out why she's so sad, I'm going to kiss all the pain away.

After I take my turn in the bathroom we climb into bed, and I pull her into my arms. "Tell me," I whisper.

"The cottage will be sold. And my parents have to move to Canada."

This last bit is unexpected. "That's kind of extreme," I whisper. "The presidency is only four years."

She sighs. "It's a money issue. They don't have any."

This surprises me because I was pretty sure that her parents were both well employed. "And Canada is cheaper?"

"Apparently. Also, this cottage is their whole nest egg. They used to have piles of money. But when I was sixteen, they lost it all."

"Oh." A chill hits the back of my neck. Then it slithers right down my spine. "Why is that?" I'm asking the question, but I know exactly what she's about to say. I can feel it in my gut.

"Because of HIMCO." She sighs. "It was this local investment manager—he was famous for his terrific returns. My grandfather's trusts were there. And also my dad's retirement account. Every penny. They lost it all."

And now I can't breathe. There's an elephant sitting on my

chest. Ash is still talking, but I can't hear her because it takes a moment for my brain to catch up to what the pain in my chest already knows.

I'm going to lose Ash. For good. There is nothing I can do about it.

She was never mine to begin with.

"Braht?" she whispers. "Say something."

"I'm so sorry," I choke out. And it's the truest thing I've ever said. But I don't follow it up with an explanation. I don't tell her that HIMCO was my father's company. Honestly, a foolish part of me has always thought that maybe Ash knew it already. People talk. Some of my colleagues at VanderMollen know why I changed my last name to Braht. I thought maybe I'd get a pass. Maybe I could finally be happy and have the life I always dreamed with Ash.

She doesn't know, though. And when she finds out, that's it. I'm history.

I force air into my lungs and try to think of what to do.

"I'll be okay eventually," she says. "Earlier today I was wishing for another listing. Be careful what you wish for, right?"

Then she rolls onto my chest to kiss me. Her long legs straddle mine, and she weaves her fingers into my hair. Her perfect tits touch my chest. And then her soft lips meet mine.

And I'm...dead inside. I feel nothing. I won't let myself.

This is going to end very badly.

"Braht?" she whispers after a single kiss.

Poor Ash is confused, because right about now I should be practically humping her leg with enthusiasm. She doesn't understand why I'm not ready to lick her everywhere and bang the headboard against the wall.

I can't actually tell her. Not quite yet. Because first there's another problem to clear up, and even though my heart is breaking, I will not let her down.

"Dwight is parked around the corner from my house," I say.

"What?"

"Yeah." And then I take a deep breath for the first time since she said the word HIMCO. The oxygen is useful to my poor brain, and suddenly I know what to do. "The Dwight situation seems to be escalating. But I found a way to monitor him. And it's going to be okay."

"How?" She sits up, looking freaked.

"Listen," I whisper. "Shh."

She lies back down on my chest immediately. How horrible that she's chosen this moment to finally trust me. I stroke her hair just once so that I'll remember the feel of it later. This might be the last chance I'll ever have to hold her.

"Here's what we're going to do," I say. "I have a plan."

Ash

I let Braht drive us back to town in the morning. My eyes feel sandpapery from crying. But sometime last night I got it all out. This morning I feel clear-headed—subdued but not beaten. Cuddling all night was therapeutic. And I need to keep my wits about me if I'm going to stay clear of Dwight as well as save my parents' cottage.

Rush hour is already underway, and when I turn to see his profile, he's frowning with concentration. But I take a moment to just admire him. He's so beautiful. On the outside, yes, but also inside, and that's the part that matters most to me. Although, come on, the outside is pretty great, too. I can admit how I feel about him now. I fought my attraction to him hard because I was sure there weren't any perfect men in the world. And there aren't.

But this one is perfect for *me*.

He hired a private investigator to help him keep me safe. I am a girl who has learned to take care of herself. I would never have asked him to do that. But the fact that he did it made my cold little heart pitter patter. It's the most romantic thing anyone has ever done for me.

We were too busy whispering in the dark last night for me to reward him properly. But I'm going to find some way to show him the depths of my appreciation.

Hello, tingling nipples. Yes, I hear you. Go ahead and say I told you so.

Braht exits the highway. We're almost to Brynn and Tom's house. That's where I'll be staying the next few nights. "Not because he can't find you there," Braht explained this morning. "But because Tom is available to play bodyguard these next few days."

Meanwhile, Braht is going to keep up with Dwight's movements, with the help of the PI. They both believe that Dwight may be re-arrested for violation of his probation agreement and that the whole nightmare might just go away.

My friends are the best. And Braht is amazing. The only thing I don't like about this arrangement is that I can't wake up next to Braht tomorrow. I'll be in Brynn and Tom's spare bedroom.

The fact that Brynn will make stuffed French toast for breakfast is, however, a comfort in my sadness.

Speaking of sadness, Braht looks glum this morning. In fact, he's barely spoken at all since we got in the car.

"Are you okay?" I ask him suddenly.

A beat goes by. "Of course. I'm just a little tired."

Hmm. I'm not sure I buy it. Too tired to pinch my ass on the way down the stairs this morning? Too tired to tease me about using my family drama as an excuse to pick up one more listing before the year ends? Too tired to rib me for writing out my to-do list at my parents' table in six complementary colors?

That doesn't sound like him. He's never this quiet, either. It's definitely something to watch. "When will I see you again?" I ask.

Maybe I'm crazy, but I swear his jaw clenches. "I'm not sure. We'll play it by ear."

The answer almost sounds cold. And it would scare me, except for the words he whispered in the dark last night just as I was drifting off to sleep. "I love you, Ash. And I won't let anything bad happen to you."

Nobody has said anything like that to me in my life, except for the people who birthed me. I know that even if Braht is in a funk, everything will be okay. He told me it would be and I'm choosing to believe him

We pull up in front of Brynn's little Victorian house a couple minutes later. She comes running outside in her slippers, carrying an aerosol can. When I get out of the car, she looks up and down the street, like a secret service agent guarding the president. "Run along inside, Ash. If that motherfucker pops out of the bushes I'm going to pepper spray his ass."

"But..." She is hustling me toward the front door. "You're holding a can of olive oil spray." It's the stuff she uses in the frying pan when she's cooking her meatballs.

"He doesn't know that." She aims the aerosol can first one way down the street, and then the other.

I roll my eyes at Braht. But he doesn't smile. Instead, he steps closer to me, kisses me on the temple, and says, "Goodbye, honey bear. Take good care of yourself."

His voice is tight, and I don't like the sadness in it. But then Tom pulls up in Braht's car. He gets out and pops the trunk, revealing my suitcases. He lifts these out, tosses Braht the keys, pats him on the back, and sends Braht on his way.

"Give me a couple of days!" he calls.

The door is shut before I even get a chance to say goodbye.

"Come on, Ash," Tom says, giving me a quick hug. "Let's go inside and plan out your day. I'm at your disposal."

I'm still reeling from Braht's hasty departure. No kiss? What the fuck?

But Brynn is waving the can around and looking tense. She's so fierce and adorable looking, and my heart scrunches when I see she's got the tiniest little pooch of a belly. When she motions with her olive oil to follow them inside, I do, trying not to look back at Braht.

Ash

I swear I just walked into Willy Wonka's factory. Before me is a
sea of chocolate and gumdrop fir trees. And...is that a winter
squash full of melty, cheesy dip?

"Brynn...what the fuck?" I say it with awe, because that's the
only thing you can do when Brynn has gone on a cooking rampage
in preparation for the oncoming holidays. She and Tom have
decorated her little Victorian home for a fall bacchanal, which I'm
pretty sure will include dancing naked around a cornucopia while
eating deep-fried cheese curds.

"I may have gone a little overboard," she says. "But I've been
trying out recipes for my holiday special. We're going to shoot
it here."

That makes sense. There are colored leaf garlands on the
fireplace that actually twinkle with starlight. Tom looks proud as
he gives me the tour of his decorating efforts. There are shelves
with a tiny village that has an actual waterfall, and mini cars, and
mini dogs being walked by mini people. The fireplace is flickering
with some kind of cinnamon fire and real logs.

Then I notice that Tom is wearing a flannel shirt and jeans

and Brynn is wearing a matching flannel shirt, jeans and booties. It's like...it's like they're morphing into a young version of Mr. and Mrs. Claus. If this is what Thanksgiving looks like, what the fuck is going to happen during Christmas? Am I going to enter an actual working North Pole? Are there going to be tiny elves to greet me? This is terrifying! Little elves! Brynn making gingerbread. Tom building a sleigh!

"Are you okay?" Brynn asks. "You're hyperventilating."

I look at her and blink a few times. She must be told. "I've had a glimpse of your Christmas future and you need to shut that shit down."

She laughs. "Don't worry. This is just for the Thanksgiving show. Although you should see our plans for the Christmas episode..."

And with that, Tom whips out actual blueprints, unfurls them on the counter and starts explaining. Brynn hands me some butterbeer. I look around in case there's some tiny person with pointy ears about to put slippers on my feet.

Goddamn, it's comforting in here. I could almost forget about all the stress in my life. Almost. But not quite.

While Tom discusses a manger scene he's crafting from birch branches, I nod appreciatively. But I'm privately planning my own to-do list. And it's a doozy.

My parents have been saints. When I think of how hard they've worked in giving me a good home, and helping me after the Dweeb disaster, I get all misty eyed. I don't want them to have to lose the cottage, too. It's good for our family. To be honest, it's good for me.

Tom is still talking, but I can't focus. Either it's the butterbeer or I'm having a Eureka moment. That's like an orgasm for your brain. And there's no stimulation required. Also there's no orgasm, so as good as a Eureka! is, there's no toe-curling.

My Eureka is this: I can save the cottage. I totally can.

I'm nodding really enthusiastically and I hope Tom doesn't realize it's not for him or for the three-tiered Christmas scene he's going to build with moveable parts. No. It's because my parents are selling our cottage, our dear sweet cottage, so they can have money to retire. I can sell the shit out of that house. I can sell it faster than any house I've sold before. In fact, I'm selling it right this very minute.

That's when the Eureka shudders through my body.

I'm going to *buy* the cottage. Me! I just won't tell my parents I'm their buyer until I've pulled it off.

It won't be easy. The first step will be to put my boring, cold house up for sale. The real estate market in Grand Rapids has been booming, especially because millennials are aching to put down roots and brew their own beer by growing hops.

My backyard is right on the bike trail, which is almost as good as having an acre for hops.

So, I'll sell it, which won't be hard. I can rent a tiny studio apartment and curtail all my shopping. It won't be very nice, but that's okay. In the summer I can stay at my parents' cottage, which will stay in the family where it belongs. After my dad retires to Canada, we'll have summers together, and I won't miss them so much.

This will be hard, but I can do it.

I'm awash with inspiration and good cheer. I will make this happen, and then I will celebrate with Braht in front of the fireplace at the cottage, with the waves in the background. I picture a jar of honey, a bearskin rug, and a saxophone. Or something. I don't know. I'm just brainstorming here, and smiling all the while. I think I even giggle and I am not a natural giggler.

Somewhere in the house, a bell rings. An angel either got its wings, or I've got some control back again. It feels good, being in control. My hard nipples seem to agree.

"So what do you think?" Brynn asks. I realize Tom has finished his spiel and they're both looking at me expectantly. I am a bad friend. Bad, bad friend. So I try: "Yes?" hoping that's vague enough and yet supportive of whatever they've just told me.

"Great!" Tom says and actually claps me on the back. "I'll get started. You can help me with some power tools."

Hmm. I wish I knew what I'd just agreed to do.

"While we're waiting for him to get set up, we can work on this," Brynn says and then puts something hard and firm in my hand. I'm afraid to look down. "I'm going to go throw up for a second," she says cheerfully. "But as soon as I get back, we can start hot-gluing the shit out of things!"

She scampers out of the kitchen and I realize it's worse than I feared. I'm holding a glue gun and there's a bucket of sequins placed in front of me.

Sequins.

Where is Braht when I need him? And I really need him...now.

23 MAKE IT SEXY

Ash

I cannot speak of what just happened. I must not speak about it. I feel too traumatized. It involved Christmas music—in November—Tom hammering things together, which resulted in Brynn getting hot and bothered.

And I hot-glued my thumbs together. That's gonna leave a mark. The upside is that Tom decided he didn't trust me with his power tools after that.

It's been about seven hours since Tom became my bodyguard, and I've had just about all I can take. Nothing dangerous will happen to me. Dwight is nowhere nearby and, honestly, I'm sick of even the idea of him controlling my life.

Enough is enough.

"I need to go home," I tell Brynn and Tom. "I'm afraid any minute you two are going to go put on matching sweaters and I'll spontaneously combust. Poof!"

"So...Ash will be...ash?" Tom asks. Then he chuckles like a dork.

He just made a dad joke! Things are worse than I thought.

"Right." I stand up in a hurry. I have to get out of here, stat.

"Really, guys, thank you for an amazing day of food and holiday, but I need to get back to my little room of white walls."

We all pause and think about that for a second.

"That doesn't sound right," I say. "I just need to get home and do some...stuff."

Brynn looks me up and down and then says, "No."

"No! Noooo? Why?"

Brynn and Tom share a look. I hate when couples Share A Look. It's never good when that happens. Either they're going to start making out in front of me or worse.

"Look," Tom says, "Braht asked me specifically to keep an eye on you. Just for the weekend. He's got...some...things...he's working on. It's important." There's something about Tom's voice that's not very Tom-like.

"What do you mean?"

"I mean...look. You know how Braht is pretty cocky all the time? Sort of annoying? Stuck up? Facetious?"

"Yeah," I say, nodding. We all know this.

"He wasn't any of those things when he asked me to help out. He was 100% serious. It sorta scared the shit out of me."

I let that sink in. That is scary. But there are things I need to do.

"If I can find someone big and burly to hang out with me, would that be okay? Just to give you two a break? I'll come back tomorrow morning, bright and early, okay?"

There's that Shared Look again. "Big and burly?" asks Brynn. "I thought you and Braht were a thing now. Like, a happy thing. A together thing."

"We are," I say confidently. "I'm going to call his brother." When I register her look of panic, I reassure her. "His brother and I don't have anything going. Really. One, his brother is gay, and two, I'm pretty much sure I'mfallinginlovewithBraht." I say the last part really hushed and fast-like, so maybe they missed it.

Tom is grinning like Brynn just flashed him and he threw beads at her.

They didn't miss that last part.

"Okay, then," Tom says and Brynn nods. "Give Bramly a call."

I text Bramly, but I'm hoping that Braht returns the call, not his brother.

No such luck, though.

Where is Braht, anyway? I'm equally annoyed with Braht's disappearance as I am at myself for wondering about it. Just as soon as I allow myself to fall in love I start questioning and overanalyzing every little thing...

My phone rings, saving me from more of this circular thinking. It's Bramly calling me back immediately, and we arrange to meet.

Tom drives me to my place and we're met by tall, handsome Bramly, the younger version of Braht. And he's got his camera with him. This is good. This is what I want.

"So, you want me to take pictures of your house?" Bramly asks.

"Yes." I nod, hoping I don't have to explain further.

"Care to explain?"

Shit. "Because I want to create a photo album of my house so I can always remember it?" I ask.

His eyes go all scrunchy.

I give in. "Because I'm selling it." I wait to see if he's going to ask more questions, but he shrugs and says "Cool. I just wanted to know what kind of lighting to apply and which lens. If you're trying to sell it, then I have to rein in my artistic tendencies."

"Is that going to be a problem?"

He takes a deep cleansing breath and shakes out his shoulders. "Let me channel my most commercial muse, and I think we'll be fine."

"This is a paid gig," I point out quickly. "And if the house looks great on the MLS website, I can find you more customers."

"Yeah?" His eyes widen. I can almost see dollar signs in them.

He and Braht do share a gene pool after all. Go figure.

"Sell my house, LittleBraht. Make it sexy. And all my clients will want you to do the same for them."

"Sexy, huh?"

"Well, within reason." Maybe I'm playing with fire. "No naked people in the shots," I clarify.

He sighs. "If you insist." And then he's off, moving about the space, muttering to himself. He takes the lens cap off his camera and begins framing shots.

I glance around, wondering what he sees. I didn't really have to tidy up, because I'm already a very organized person. Honestly, if a buyer walked in that door right now, she might assume I don't even live here.

And maybe there's some truth to that. This house was an investment. It has always been a temporary place for me, somewhere to sleep and eat until I found what I was really looking for.

Until now, I didn't even realize I was searching. It's funny, the power of your subconscious.

I should be at the cottage right now, putting that on the market first. And I will make that happen. But putting *this* house on the market doesn't make me feel emotional. Not like the cottage does.

Ergo, the next thing I have to do won't be hard. I grab my laptop, brew some coffee and start typing away. *Location, location! 3BR, 2 bath, quiet street. Right on the jogging path!* And since I'm a realtor, I don't even have to look up the comps. I already know the right price. In less than half an hour I've written up my little house's listing and saved it to *drafts*.

However. Writing a listing for the cottage takes longer.

Make family memories in an adorable 3BR craftsman-style cottage with sweeping views of Lake Michigan. Lovely. Homey. You don't deserve this place. STAY AWAY.

Just kidding.

Sort of.

I feel nauseated just listing the cottage at all. But I have to do it in order to keep up the ruse. I'll list it on the MLS and then call my parents immediately to tell them I have an offer on the cottage already.

It won't even really be a lie. I will have an offer. They just won't know it's from me.

There are sounds coming from the guest bedroom. I hear a sensual sigh, and I wonder what the heck Bramly is up to in there. On tiptoe, I make my way toward the room and peer around the door frame.

And it's beautiful. Bramly has styled the bed like a promo shot for a B&B. He's removed a throw pillow from my sofa and placed it just so on the bed. The covers are turned down on one side. And one of the silk roses I keep in a vase has been positioned on the pillow. Only it's...sexual somehow. The angle of the rose against the pillow looks somehow debauched. Like it's taking a post-coital snooze before round two.

Wow.

Either Bramly is a subtle genius, or I'm sexually frustrated. It could really go either way.

He takes a dozen or so absolutely perfect shots of my boring little house. I actually have to pry him away from the half bathroom. "I need a wider angle lens," he frets. "I could make it look like those hand towels are enraptured..."

"Come on, Romeo," I prod. "I need you to take a drive with me to our lake cottage."

"You do? Will I get to take some more photos?"

"No." I shake my head.

"Why not? Didn't you say you were putting it on the market?"

"I am. But these photos need to suck. So I'm taking them with my phone."

He recoils. "Let me get this straight. You want me to go and *watch* while you take a bunch of shitty pics with your phone? Why would I do that?"

"You're just the bodyguard in this situation. And I'll still compensate you for your time and try to find you more clients."

He chews his aristocratic lip. "Okay, fine. But I have two conditions."

"Which are?" I can't wait to hear this.

"One"—he holds up a finger—"you don't use any cheesy Instagram filters on your shots. My stomach couldn't take it. And, two, I pick out something for you to wear from your closet, and you let me take a picture of you when the sun is setting. At the beach. Christmas is coming and I want to give my brother something special."

"A picture of me is something special?"

"You're all he's ever wanted." Bramly smiles.

Then where is he? my heart wonders.

After our photo shoot at the cabin, I ask Bramly to take me back to Braht's house.

"I thought you were staying at Tom's?"

"That's what your brother said, but it's not what I want. Ergo, take me to Casa Braht."

"Yes, ma'am," Bramly chuckles. "I like it when you boss my brother around."

"Why?"

"Because somebody should."

"Well, it's my pleasure." You know, I like Bramly. He's a weird bird. Then again so is his brother.

Apparently I have a thing for weird men.

When Bramly pulls up in front of my man's house, it's suppertime. I pay Bramly in cash for his time, and he's smiling when he drives away.

As I approach Casa Braht, the door swings open. My man is standing there, looking down his aristocratic nose at me. "You're supposed to be with Brynn and Tom," he says.

"Hey." I pull up short. "In the first place, that's no way to greet a lady. And in the second place, you told me to stay at Brynn and Tom's. But I didn't *agree*."

His jaw hardens. "Well, you should. It's for your own good."

And just like that I'm back to remembering every off-putting thing Braht ever said. Every irritating detail of our past conflicts rises up in me like a bad case of hives. "Do you even hear yourself right now? It's *my life*, you big mansplainer. I can walk around without the protection of a male chromosome if I damn well feel like it." I climb the steps and open the screen door.

He jumps back to let me in, but his eyes are an extra-chilly shade of blue. And I feel the cold like a snake of worry down my spine.

"Did you have a bad day or something?" I prompt. Maybe there's a simple explanation for his shitty reaction to me showing up at his front door.

"The worst," he admits with a sigh.

Ah, well then. I'm thinking we could fight some more and then have makeup sex. Or maybe just skip right to the sex. "Can I make it better?"

His face softens. "The thing is, you really can't." I wait for him to elaborate, but he doesn't. "Let's eat. I'll make dinner." He turns away.

I'm still so very confused. Also, I haven't been kissed hello. That's disturbing. But I follow him to the kitchen and sit on a bar stool while he begins to pull things out of the refrigerator. He puts on an apron and begins to shred chicken onto a plate.

So I tell him about my big plan to buy the cottage. And about the listing I wrote for my little house, too.

He drops a pan roughly onto the stove, then curses.

"What's the matter?" It's pretty unusual to see him lose his cool.

"Just, uh." He sighs. "I don't think you should put your house on the market." His long fingers lay tortillas onto a skillet.

"Why not? I have to sell. Quickly, too."

"Just...don't, okay?"

All the hairs stand up on the back of my neck. "I wasn't asking to move in with you, I swear."

I meant it as a joke, but he looks up from the pan and our eyes meet. His are troubled. And now there's a little pain in my belly where there wasn't before. He thinks I was angling to move in with him. I totally wasn't. It's too soon.

And good thing, right? Because I just learned that Braht hates this idea. A lot.

Now I feel hurt for no reason at all.

And he's on the other side of the bar, making some kind of chicken lime tacos with crumbled cheese. "Would you crack open a couple of beers?" he asks.

"Sure," I whisper. But then I just sit there and stare at him for a minute longer.

"They're in the door," he prompts.

I want to kick him. But instead I cross to the fridge and remove two beers. They're Mexican, so I find a lime to cut up, too. Those are in the fruit drawer. Everything is perfect at Casa Braht. Except he isn't looking at me like he wants to jump me anymore. And I don't know what to do with that.

I set the beers and the lime down on the counter. "Sebastian?"

"What?" The sound of his real name brings his gaze around to mine.

"Are you mad at me for some reason? Did I do something wrong?"

He blinks. "No, Ash. Not a thing." He flips a tortilla with a shiny spatula. "You're perfect."

"Then why are you all the way over there when I'm over here?"

Braht sighs. He turns off the heat under the griddle and walks slowly around to stand beside me. I can smell his aftershave. His sweater looks soft, and I want to run my hand over his chest. I want to lay my face on his shoulder and be held.

But I don't. There's an invisible force field separating us right now, and I don't know how it got there.

He leans in and places his forehead against mine. "I just have a lot on my mind, okay?"

"Okay," I whisper. But it's not okay. "I think something is bothering you, and you won't tell me what."

He straightens up again, then heads for the cabinet with the plates inside. "I think you're very astute."

"So lay it on me, okay? I can take it."

He turns around looking sadder than I've ever seen him look. "Two tacos or three?"

"Braht," I demand. "Tell me your feelings."

"I wouldn't want to lose my man card," he says, tossing warmed tortillas onto each plate.

"Hey. I was wrong about that," I say.

"Maybe not," he says quietly.

We eat dinner together, but it's strained. I want to cry. I want to rage. But I don't do either one. You can't make a man confide in you. You can't make a man love you.

I've tried.

Later, after some TV watching that isn't as cuddly as I wished, I decide to turn in first. "I'll be reading," I announce. "It's an erotica book. It's teaching me things."

His face gives a twitch.

I start to head up the stairs, trailing my hand on the banister like it's oh so hard and firm. Up and down. Silently hoping it doesn't give me a splinter because it's really hard to be sexy when you're screaming, "OH MY GOD I HAVE A SPLINTER."

I sex up my voice a little. Make it lower. A little like Lauren Bacall. I say: "This book is downright inspirational. It's made me see the possibilities. You know, of handing over the reins to you in the bedroom. I was going to let you earn your man card back. And I'm pretty sure licking will be involved. Also, a ping-pong paddle. Maybe."

I glide up the stairs and don't turn around to see if Braht is watching me.

Of course he is. I can hear him panting from a mile away.

24 PEDICURES AND PLANS

Braht

I will not have sex with Ash.

I will not make love to Ash.

I *can't*. Not without telling her that I wrecked her parents' retirement. Well, my parents did. But I actually aided and abetted them.

My parents prevented me from telling anyone that they'd left town, and I went along with it. They were able to transfer all their ill-gotten gains into an account in the Caymans, and all because I did just what they asked.

If not for my silence, every bilked investor would have gotten at least a small percentage of his investment back.

Ash will never forgive me.

That's why I will not allow myself to imagine Ash on her hands in knees on the bed, naked, looking back at me, her long blonde hair cascading to the bed, her beautiful ass all round and firm, waiting for me to lick and taste and thrust into gently at first, and then with more force until I'm balls deep and she's crying out my name, my real name, and I lean over and grab her tits...

And...

I am up those stairs before I can connect my brain to my body. My body has its own mind right now and it's yelling "*ASH!*" She spins around to look at me and I push her up against the wall.

When did she put this silky nightgown on? Wait—who cares? All I care about is kissing her and running my tongue all over her body. Pinning her arms above her head and just tasting her everywhere. Her nipples are so hard. I can see them through the silky fabric and I don't even brush the fabric away, I just suck one nipple into my mouth, wetting the silk around her until it's see-through. Then I move to the other one because lefty will be jealous. But also because I have to have my mouth on every part of her.

She tugs my head upward, trying to kiss me. "Don't *move*, honey bear." It comes out sounding gruffer than I mean it to. We take a second to look at each other and she—I don't know how to explain it. I see a shift in her eyes. She *trusts* me. She knows I have only her pleasure on my mind, and she actually waits patiently for me to instruct her on what to do next.

"Turn around," I say. The control she's given me is heady stuff. I'll make sure not to take advantage of it.

She turns, and I run my hands down her curves, to the bottom of her silky chemise. In one long pull I've got that thing off her, and Ash is naked in my hallway, save for the heels she's wearing. God*damn*. She's beautiful. Her body is a sleek hourglass. She's shaped like a violin, and I want to play her.

I skim my hands down again, this time over bare skin. She lets out a whimper as I pull her close to me. My hard cock lines up against her ass. I reach around and just embrace her while I kiss the side of her neck. Then I turn her around again.

It's sort of like a dance. I lead with a little pressure of my hand, and she follows. And I realize that this isn't about me being in control in the bedroom. It never has been. It's just about her trusting me. No—strike that. It's us trusting each other.

I drop to my knees.

That's what you do when you worship someone. Or you're, you know, Elvis and you've reached a dramatic part in your song. Whatever.

She leans against the wall and I nudge her legs apart. I tenderly lift her foot and place it over my shoulder so that I can have better access to the very core of her.

She moans and that's all I need. I press my tongue between her legs. She shifts a little, giving me a deeper angle while I lick and probe. I am all lips and tongue and I am insatiable. "Oh," she gasps. "Oh, fuck." Her heel scratches my back, and her hand threads through my hair and tugs. Her panting alone is almost enough to make me come, but I hold back because I want to be deep inside her before I let go.

I want her to let go with me. "Are you close?" I ask.

"Very," she breathes.

So I pull away. I will never get enough of her. I need hours and days and years. "On the bed," I say.

She ducks past me and into the bedroom. By the time I clear the corner a moment later, she's on the bed on her knees, just like I'd envisioned. I let out an "*Ungh*." The view is even more perfect than I thought possible.

Just...wow. She waits, facing away from me. And somehow that's even sexier than a hot stare.

As I approach I can see the remnant of an old tattoo on her bum. I just cover it with the palm of my hand. I use my other hand to nudge her thighs apart. "Honey bear, I want you so bad right now." I ease my hand between her legs.

She's wet and ready for me, and she moans as I dip a finger inside. "Too many words," she pants. "Too many clothes."

It takes me ten seconds to fix the clothes issue, but even that feels like too long to be away from her. While I'm undressing, she grabs a condom from my side table and rips it open with her teeth. Then I take a step toward her, my dick at full mast, ready to be sheathed. "You do it," I bark.

She turns and sheathes me with eager hands and hungry eyes.

"Good girl," I whisper. "Turn around now."

She hurries to comply. She's on all fours, her ass tilted at just the right angle.

I want to go slow. I do. I want to savor every second, but once I've got the head of my cock inside her, I'm lost. I slide all the way home.

For a moment time stops. Sound stops. The earth stops spinning. We're breathing at the same time, our bodies one and in unison. I break out in a sweat because it's so good and I'm so damned eager for her. But I hold firmly to her hips for one more beat. The anticipation is killing us both.

"Please," she whispers. It's just one word, but it does me in. I rock back and then thrust inside her.

Her moan is everything.

And that's all the patience I have. Yanking her hips back against me, I begin to fuck her in earnest. I don't stop until we're sweat covered, slippery, trembling with need. Then I feel her shivering, and the sound of her climax pushes me over the edge.

Is it the best orgasm of my life?

Fuck, yes.

Especially because we cry out at the same time. I really feel like we should get an award for that. A ribbon. A plaque maybe. Something we can hang on the wall and marvel at later.

But I'm too tired to do anything but crawl under the blankets with her and fall into a deep sleep. Our limbs are tangled together, like we're meant to be here. As if this were meant to be an everyday thing, and not the last time.

When I wake up, she's still wrapped around me and I give her a little snuggle. Then it hits me all at once. This is the last time. How could Ash ever forgive me? My father took everything from her parents. And I helped.

My sudden attack of loneliness is like getting kicked in the balls. Have you ever been kicked in the nuts? No? Well, when it happens, your balls get hoovered back into your body to protect them and your stomach turns inside out because man, that shit hurts. It's a terrible feeling, but it does pass eventually.

What I'm feeling now? It's much worse.

The kick I've taken is mental, not physical. And I'm afraid the pain will never pass. I know Ash needs me to smile at her and be the same fashionably dressed goofball I always show her. But I just can't. I'm still mentally rolling on the floor, holding a hand over my crotch.

Reality makes it impossible to stay in bed. I get up to make us a nice Western omelet and make the coffee.

When Ash comes downstairs, my greeting is tepid. I know this, but I can't seem to do better. Ash spends our breakfast time giving me sideways glances and biting her lip.

Then I drive her to the office. Before she gets out of the car, I take care to extract a promise that she won't wander the city unaccompanied. She rolls her eyes, but says she'll stay with people.

"Take care of yourself," I try to say, but it feels like there's something stuck in my throat.

She looks me over with worried eyes. "You do the same, okay?" She reaches across the car and cups my cheek.

And suddenly there's nowhere to run. The heat of her hand melts a little of this crusty exterior I'm trying so hard to maintain. And when I look back at her, I can't hold back what I'm feeling. I manage to keep my mouth shut, but I'm sure my face tells everything. I love her and we're never going to be a couple. Not in the way I want. I can't shut down my expression. I just gaze at her and let that shit fly.

Ash leans closer and I kiss her. Just one, nice, slow one. My eyes burn because it might be the last kiss I ever get. Once she learns the truth about who I am, she won't want a thing to do with me.

She pulls away on a sigh. "Will I see you tonight?"

"No," I say, clearing my throat. "I promised Bramly I'd go to some art opening of his friend's." This is actually true, but I'm probably going to bail. Instead, I'll spend the night with a bottle of Scotch, playing the Jeff Buckley version of "Hallelujah."

Real men cry sometimes. You just have to let that shit out, you know?

Ash bites her lip again. Then she gets out of my car, shuts the door, and disappears inside the office.

———

I spend the morning working from home. Like Ash, I too have a plan for how to fix her family's financial woes. She shouldn't have to do it herself.

It takes some setting up, but I'm almost ready to move on it.

Around noon I fix myself an avocado toast and eat it standing up at the counter, like a heathen. Then I wander my house with my teacup trying to decide which furniture I'll keep and which I'll probably give away.

This place is too big for me anyway. Now that Bramly lives on his own, and Ash will soon know the truth, I just don't need three bedrooms, a den and a giant garage with a man cave overhead.

Maybe I'll leave Michigan altogether. This town has been causing me various kinds of heartache for years. I don't want to live in a place where I'll always be glancing around for Ash, wondering whether she'll turn up at Bistro Bella Vita with her new boyfriend on her arm.

Man, am I broody or what? Clearly I need to get out of the house and get out of my own head. So I hightail it to the one place I go when I need some instant therapy: Nailed It, my favorite pedicure spot.

People laugh at me for coming here. But what they don't realize is how many clients I pick up in nail salons. This place should be crawling with realtors. Where else can you relax, take excellent care of your feet and hear the latest gossip about who's getting divorced and who's died?

Life events are just real estate transactions with Hallmark cards attached to them. Cynical but true.

When I walk inside, the bells on the door tinkle in time with a chorus of "*Sebastian!*"

"Hi, girls!" I wave at the regular cast of misfits. Today I spot at least five of my closest octogenarian girlfriends, wiggling and bouncing in the automatic massage chairs. I should've guessed they'd be here. It's Wednesday, and that's when the bus from Clark Retirement Home brings them to the salon and then to the grocery store.

I'm immediately comforted by the smell of acetone, the sound of bubbling water, and Bella, the Slavic commander telling me in her thick Russian accent to "Sit. Now. Do it."

Ahhh. To be told what to do. It reminds me of Ash. God, I love bossy women.

I stoop to roll my pants while Bella studies me. "You want polish today?" she barks at me.

The octogenarians giggle, because this is a schtick I have with Bella.

"Not today," I say as always. Then I stage-whisper to the ladies. "I'm getting mauve the next time. Saving it for a special occasion."

Pearl smiles wide and says, "Go with coral. It's more your color." Pearl is the feisty one of the group.

"Enough," says Bella and she points to the water. I salute and sit down. It feels...so good. I sort of just sink into the chair and exhale. Bella starts to work me over. She's very militant in her approach to my feet.

"Your feet look bad. You not take care. I tell you to come in once a week! You a slacker."

"I know, sweet Bella, but I've been busy."

"No! Never too busy for pedicure. That is failure talking."

I nod because she's right.

She shoves my feet in the hot water and then aggressively begins smoothing down my calluses. The bubbling water allows my thoughts to drift a bit.

But I'm not truly relaxed. I've given myself two days to do... what? Fix everything. My parents not only ruined mine and Bramly's childhood with their pyramid scheme, but they ruined countless others. I can't make amends to all of them. I don't know who they are, but I can help the Powers.

Isn't it just the universe laughing at me to make the one person on the planet I'm head over heels for, be the one person I'll never be able to love once she finds out the truth?

"What is wrong with you." Bella says. She tends not to ask questions. She likes statements much more. "You not being fun Braht. You being serious and whiny Braht."

It's like seeing an unforgiving therapist. "I've got something on my mind," I say.

"Tell it." She gives my feet a sharp shove. She's not asking me to tell her what's on my mind, she's ordering me to.

Pearl says, "You better say something or we're going to start talking about how many of us have had moles removed lately." There's a chorus of "I have," and I'm a little bit terrified.

So I tell them the whole thing. I tell them about my deep fascination and love for Ash, how we've connected, how when I look at office supplies now I feel frisky.

Then I tell them how my parents were terrible people and abandoned me but also ruined Ash's life. I tell them about Dweeb. That fucker. I can't help but get a little angry about that. I tell them the whole story.

"So I'm going to lose her," I say after it all tumbles out. "But I can't let her go until this fuckwad she used to be married to is rearrested."

That's the end of the story. I take a deep breath and wait.

There's a lot of blinking. Everyone looks at Bella for her words of wisdom.

"You are being, how do you say...?" She strokes her mustache. "You are being a pussy."

There's a kind of stunned silence, but then Maura at the end, petite, kindly Maura, whispers, "Actually, being a pussy is a good thing now. We've taken back that word. I think Braht needs to be more like pussy. Dark and mysterious and oh so very powerful."

There is a collective "Ahhh!" and everyone nods.

"Okay, yes!" Bella agrees. "Good. You need to stop being so whiny and be more powerful like a pussy."

I'm trying to process all of this. I really am.

Bella is still thinking hard. So hard she's stopped buffing my toes for a bit, and she's holding one of my feet in a tight grip. "You need to be more like, oh, what was that movie? It was movie that convinced me to come to America? He wears a bandana. He carries big gun. He no take shit from no one." I have no idea what to answer, but it turns out I don't have to. She snaps her fingers. "Rambo! You need to be strong like Rambo pussy, and not whiny like tiny Braht."

Goddammit.

This is some of the weirdest advice I've ever received. But I think there's some truth in there. "You have a unique way of looking at the world, you know?"

"Just truth," she snarls.

I fucking love this place.

A pair of soft hands touches my arm, and I look down to see Pearl has gotten out of her seat and approached me. "Here you go," she says and hands me a knitted pink scarf. "You tie that around your head like a Rambo bandana and you go get that motherfucker!"

All the ladies are delighted by this idea. There are cheers and cat whistles.

What can I do? My octogenarian friends are gazing at me with hope in their eyes. Bella looks at me like if I refuse, she's going to throw me in the gulag.

So I tie that pink hand-knitted scarf around my head. But only for the remaining duration of my pedi. Even I have limits.

While Bella finishes up on my feet, I consider my options. There are two tasks I must accomplish. One thing is crystal clear —fix Ash's financial woes. The other thing is a little trickier. I have to discipline Dwight. I'm not going to be allowed to look after Ash anymore, that's clear. But I'll be damned if he's going to fuck with her.

I chew on that for a bit.

Ash

That evening I insist on working late at the real estate office. I'm hoping to shake all my bodyguards. But it doesn't work. Tom insists on accompanying me. At five o'clock sharp he parks his butt in Braht's desk chair, puts on a pair of headphones and commences editing video on his laptop. "You won't even know I'm here," is the last thing he says to me.

As if I could miss his big self in that chair, though. And he keeps chuckling as he works. Everything is happy-happy-joy-joy in Tom and Brynn's life right now, and I'm glad for them. Brynn deserves her happiness.

Maybe I'll deserve mine, too, once I shake off my spoiled only-child woes and fulfill my duty.

Two hours ago I published the MLS listing with the cottage on it, then sent the link to my parents. The photos are unflattering, but everything else is ship shape. I need the listing to be real but not so appealing that we get a flood of interest immediately. The season is on my side. People don't shop for beach houses in late November. The holidays aren't great in real estate.

Now it's time to shift the plan into high gear. I take a deep breath and let it out. Lying has never been fun for me, so this won't come easily. Stalling, I line up my stapler with my pencil sharpener and check the order of my pens. None of my office supplies are having sex, which means we're all having a dry spell. Maybe that's why I'm in such a low mood.

That and the life-changing call I'm about to make.

I lift the handset and dial. Finally. It rings twice before my mother answers. "Hi sweetie! Still at work? Have you eaten?"

Aw. She's always been the kind of mom who looks after me. Now I can finally return the favor. "I ate," I promise her. "Brynn fed me a burrito. Did you get a chance to look at the listing?"

"I did." She sighs. "Thank you for doing this. It was hard to see our beautiful home for sale."

"I know."

"Everything looks fine. Those pictures don't really put everything in the best light, though."

"Well." I give a nervous giggle. "They were meant to be temporary until I could get a real camera in there. But I was calling to tell you something important. We have an offer already."

"*Really.*" The word comes out breathy. "Oh, I'm not ready!"

"I know, Mom." It's going to be okay, but I can't tell her that. "It's just a little discount to your offer price. So it's a pretty good offer. And since I found the buyer myself, that means you would save a hundred percent of the commission."

She's silent for a long moment. "I'll tell your father," she whispers.

"Okay." *Don't take too long*, I want to urge. "It's a good offer. You think about it."

"You mean..." She swallows. "We should probably take it."

"Probably," I say. "The buyer will put twenty-five percent down, so the odds of the sale going through are pretty good. She doesn't need to close immediately, either. Springtime would be fine with this buyer." *Because this buyer needs to sell her house lickety-split.*

"Right," my mom says tightly. "I need a night to get used to the idea."

"Of course," I say quickly. "I'll email you the precise terms she laid out. Take a breath, Mom. Talk to Dad. Have a glass of wine. It's going to be okay."

"Thank you, sweetie. Thank you for all your help."

"My pleasure," I say, because it really is. I would do anything for them. They helped me start over once before. I can start over again for them. I can rent a shoebox somewhere or—if absolutely necessary—look at *roommate wanted* listings.

I'll do it for them.

We hang up and I shut my computer down for the night. I nudge Tom to tell him that I'm ready to go. And while he finishes up his work, I open my planner and choose a color theme for the day. It's yellow and spring green. Sunny colors, for the sunny outlook that I will grab onto with both hands.

I could add, in script, *Today is the first day of the rest of my life.* But I don't, because *please*, bitch. Motivation is everything—but motivational quotes with butterflies above them are tacky.

Tom and I are just standing up to go when Dennie gallops in the front door. Usually he's more of a shuffler, but not today. He's so excited he practically whinnies. "Ash!" he yells, charging toward me.

Tom slides his big body in front of mine and says, "Who's looking for her?"

Dennie pulls up short. "Uh, I could come back?" He looks at both of us and then quickly says, "But I have an offer on her property. They wanted to deal just with me. Me! A real bona fide offer, from some very important people. They're foreign!"

For one fraction of a second, my heart soars. Because it's in my DNA to get excited whenever someone says, "I have an offer." "Very important people" is good, too.

But then I remember what it's for, and my stomach drops. "Wait, really?" I say, sidestepping Tom. "You have an offer on the beach cottage?" Inside I say, "MY cottage?"

"Sure do!" He beams. "Right at the asking price."

I won't panic yet, because an asking price offer isn't high enough to derail me. My parents would have to pay Dennie a commission, so his offer is still actually worse than my lower one. It's close, but no cigar, as they say. "Well done, Dennie," I say, trying to make it enthusiastic, but mostly I think I just sound constipated. "I'll let the clients know. You'll hear from us later tonight, maybe."

"Awesome!" he says. Then he trots back outside.

When the door shuts, I let out a groan.

"What's the problem?" Tom asks.

"Nothing, really. It's great," I say with the phoniest of smiles. The problem is that Dennie has just screwed up my easy sale. I can feel it in my gut. Where there's one offer, there's more.

Tom takes me back to Brynn's place. We eat dinner together—spaghetti and meatballs.

Then I call Dennie and gently inform him that the sellers have a better offer.

"Oh, blast," he says. "Let me check in with them. Maybe we can improve."

Shit.

With that done, now all I have to do is sit here alone and worry.

Tom and Brynn are putting a set together for their Christmas special. I don't really understand why they need one, but they're in the garage and there's the sound of giggling and things banging around. I'm pretty sure the "banging around" is just good old-fashioned banging. It's why I turn up the music and pour myself a gallon of sauvignon blanc. I need to crunch some numbers.

And those numbers are not crunching the way I want them to.

I just don't have enough money to improve my offer on the house very much. Unless my own place sold quickly, there simply isn't any wiggle room. If I cash in my one and only CD, I can add another 3k to my offer. I pray that it's enough.

I'm sure the other won't offer any more. I mean, sight unseen, and with those terrible pictures. I'll just tell this bidder that the sellers are accepting another offer.

But when I get him on the phone, that's not how things go. "It's unbelievable!" Dennie cries, and my stomach starts to sink before he gets the rest out. "They've added twenty-five grand to the offer! Can you believe it? This is so exciting. If you close in the spring, they won't even need a loan."

Twenty-five grand? It's the kiss of death for me. I can't compete. If I empty my account, if I sell all of my furniture, it still won't be enough.

Though this is a great deal for my parents. They'll get a nice chunk of money to buy their dream retirement condo.

But I've just lost the last bit of constancy in my life. It feels really lonely.

"It's great," I tell Dennie. I know I sound fake, but I can't help it. I'm doing the best I can here. "Offer accepted." I hang up while Dennie is screaming with pure joy.

I take a big ol' sip of my wine and just burst into tears.

Braht

"You've reached Hank Miller," the voicemail message says. I take a deep breath, preparing for a long and confusing message. Then I hear, "This is Hank Miller. You called me, Braht. What do you need? Is that fucker messing with you? I've got some people who could deal with him. I could do some outsourcing."

Huh. Not a message at all. "Ah. Outsourcing! Good idea."

He grunts. "Yeah. I went to this CEO retreat where everyone had to do trust falls and write up action plans. My takeaway was that I needed to outsource more often. Busting up people's faces doesn't have a good rate of investment for me currently."

I'm not sure how to respond. "No, I don't need his face busted. Mostly I'm looking for advice."

"Okay. Shoot." I swear I can hear him lean back in his squeaky office chair and take a deep drink of Scotch. And is that the faint sound I hear of a saxophone solo in the distance? He's classic detective noir.

"I'm still able to track him and I think I want to approach him."

"Approach him?" Hank sounds genuinely baffled. "But not to bust his face?"

"No. I was thinking more of making a deal between two gentlemen. If he lays off Ash, then I won't...I don't know exactly."

"You won't turn over a heap of evidence I've uncovered for you that will get his tweedle dick put back in jail?"

That's quite the suggestion. "You are a prince among men, Hank."

He snorts. "Look, you wanted my advice. If you approach this guy, grab onto his balls like you're trying to make a pancake sandwich, rough up his face, give him a wedgie, wrap him up all Christmas-y in duct tape, and then you throw his ass in jail. Preferably after you've set him on fire."

"Well..."

"Too gruesome for you? You could always outsource it."

Hank is full of good ideas. "Not really my style."

There's an awkward silence. Then Hank says, "Or you could play it your way. Be all friendly like. Make a gentlemanly deal with him. I just have one word of warning for you."

"Okay. What's that?"

"That Dwight Engersoll ain't no gentleman."

"I will keep that in mind."

"Watch for the email I'm sending over. It's full of evidence. And have a great Christmas!" Hank says and ends the call.

———

An hour later, I've parked my car and I'm bundled up in my Burberry coat and Icelandic scarf. I've followed the dot on my phone app into a seedier part of downtown Grand Rapids. It's a formerly industrial area down by the arena, with bumpy streets and bad lighting.

But the parking is super cheap. So I've got that going for me.

Dwight's car is parked outside of a noodle shop called Pho

Queue. I stare up at the sign and try to decide whether or not the shop owner knows how that sounds.

It could really go either way.

My target is easily visible just inside the nearly empty storefront. He's sitting at a bright orange table looking grumpy.

I'd planned to confront him privately, but maybe this is for the best. It's starting to snow on me out here, and it'd be really picturesque if I weren't pissed. So I decide to just get it over with, right here in the noodle shop. Besides, if Dwight turns out to be more than I can handle, the owner of Pho Queue might call 911.

Or not. When I walk inside there's only one big man behind the counter. His nose is pierced so many times I wonder how he can pass through a metal detector. Also, he looks even grumpier than Dwight.

On the plus side of things, the place smells amazing. There's a spicy, meaty scent in the air, and a hint of basil. And now I'm starving. Grief is sort of exhausting, and I really could use the calories.

"What do you want?" grunts the scary dude behind the counter.

"Spicy tonkotsu," I hear myself say. "With braised pork belly."

"Twelve fifty." The guy gives me an evil gaze that my pedicurist would envy, and then disappears in back.

Well. If I die tonight, at least I'll be well fed.

Instead of finding a table, I stand at the counter, so Dwight won't notice me. He hasn't made a sound since I walked in. I put my money on the counter and wait.

A few minutes later, this establishment's only visible employee comes back with a tray. "Not for you," he says, just in case I was about to feel any pleasure.

"Right."

He sets the tray down in front of Dwight and then returns to the kitchen. But he only keeps me waiting another two minutes. And the tray he sets down on the counter for me is mouth-watering. "Hey, thanks."

He grimaces.

Okay.

I take the tray and turn around. Dweeb is tucking into his meal. In a burst of bravery, I carry my tray over to his table and set it down opposite him. He looks up at me, the noodles spilling out of his mouth like he's Cthulhu in man-form. "Dwight!" I say. "How's it hanging?"

He slurps in response. "Low," he says. I nod and shovel some of this meaty heaven into my mouth. It actually warms me from the inside out. I'm feeling downright congenial.

We eat together for several long minutes. I don't know whether he doesn't know me or he's really just pretending. In the meantime, I'm enjoying some excellent soup.

"I know you," he says eventually.

I nod, but don't say anything, because of pho.

"Don't you bag groceries at that Martha's Vineyard deli place?"

"No," I say.

"Sure you do! You're always wearing one of those holiday sweaters you can get at Meijer!" He's excited about this.

"I assure you, I don't wear holiday sweaters from Meijer."

"Huh. Then you must be that douche that's fucking my wife."

Wait a minute! Douche? His wife? I feel a swelling and realize it's my testosterone levels. They're rising from the normal range right into Rambo territory.

"Ash is not your wife. Not anymore." It's hard to say this calmly, but I manage.

He seems to deflate a little and pushes his bowl away. I keep eating my pho just to prove he hasn't affected my appetite. This is a battle of wills and I am winning.

"Yeah, I know. I really fucked that one up. I'm not so hot on relationships, you know? My therapist says that I'm trapped in old-school patterns of hostile masculinity, and I need to break out of that. This fucking pansy had the cojones to suggest I take up knitting. Knitting, can you imagine?"

It's not a bad idea, actually. Maybe knitting would help Dwight tap into his nurturing side.

"I'm trying, man. To be better. But prison does things to you. I'm glad Ash is happy. You treating her well?"

"Yeah," I say, starting to feel like I stepped into a parallel universe where Dwight isn't a dick and actually has a heart. "But here's the thing. You need to back off."

"Back off? What do you mean?"

I don't hide my eye roll. "You've been following her. Calling her. Scaring her. Trying to approach her. That shit's got to stop." I'm done with my pho so I push my bowl away. I do this firmly. I'm channeling Jackie Chan right now, and it's working for me.

"Christ. I'm not trying to scare her. She's got something of mine. It's mine, and I need it. I've tried to talk to her with emails and then phone calls. I ran into her once in the parking lot. I just need this one thing and then she can have her life and I'll have mine."

That sounds almost reasonable. "What do you need from her? Maybe I can get it for you."

Dweeb leans back and smiles. It's an oily smile. It has charm on the surface, but I know better. Though I can totally see how Ash might've been sucked into his charm. Underneath that charm is a real, live snake, and I've just glimpsed him slithering.

And now I've had enough. Of the Pho. Of Dwight. Of this night. "I came here to give you a message, okay? You're going to back off, or I turn in the stack of evidence I have against you."

"Evidence? What evidence? Of my volunteering at the homeless shelter? Of me working cleaning carpets and being on time every day? You don't know shit." He laughs. That fucker laughs.

Then I decide to lay my cards on the table, because Dweeb is not a good guy. Not at all. "My PI photographed you going in and out of a certain pawn shop seven times in the last week."

His face twitches at that. "So what? I need a TV."

"This pawn shop is run by a mobster who has an office in

back. He followed you inside and took your picture chatting with that guy. Every few months his henchmen get thrown in jail for grand larceny, so he's always on the lookout for new meat."

Dwight makes a face like he tastes something sour. "I was asking for his advice. I got a little technical problem I need to solve, and he knows a lot about, uh, home security."

I just shrug. "The police will be very interested in these photos, right? If you come within two hundred feet of Ash, I will take a pair of chopsticks and skewer your balls, one on top of the other. And then turn you and my photos over to the cops. Are we clear?"

He actually gulps.

My work done, I stand up and wave to the big dude at the counter.

He gives me a big smile, exposing a rack of gold teeth. "Respect," he says.

Then I'm gone.

26 SPEAKING SWEDISH

Ash

The next morning I go to work with swollen eyes. Braht is not at his desk. He's avoiding me for some reason, I don't know why. I can only deal with one major life trauma at a time, so I decide to worry about that later. Today is all about the cottage.

Dennie brings me a cup of coffee and a worried glance. "Everything okay there, Ash-kicker?"

I laugh in spite of my woe. "Is that my nickname around here?"

"Well." He lets out a nervous chuckle. "That's how I think of you."

"I like it, Dennie. Good one."

He slips a document onto my desk. "Here's the official offer letter. There aren't any complicated contingencies, so I expect we'll move to contract with no real difficulty."

My stomach dips. "Thank you. I'll read this right away." He's right, too. This is a good offer. It makes no unreasonable demands and is not contingent on a mortgage or inspection.

I sip the coffee that Dennie brought me and gird my loins for the call I need to make to my parents. *I've sold the cottage for you. You got a great price.* My mother will thank me. But I'd really wanted to make an entirely different call. *I have a plan to personally save the cottage!*

But we don't always get the things we want.

It's going to take a lot of yoga classes and several spa treatments before I can feel zen about this.

I drain the coffee and reach for the phone. As I push Dennie's offer letter away from me, my eyes snag on the buyer's name. It's foreign all right, complete with an umlaut. Mr. S. B. Honungsbjörn. Something tickles my senses about this name, and I don't know why.

Maybe I'm only stalling, but I open a translation tool on the Internet anyway and type in the name. Honungsbjörn is Swedish.

And it means: Honey bear.

What the...?

Could it really mean...?

No, seriously?

I am flooded with several emotions at once. Hope. Shock. Confusion.

Oh, and rage. Because if this is a trick by Braht to save the day, I can't believe he didn't just discuss it with me first.

But if it is, some other things make sense. Is this why he's acting so strangely?

Or—am I crazy? Could this buyer be unrelated to Braht? No. Those are Braht's initials, too. Mr. S.B. Honungsbjörn deliberately deceived me.

"Dennie!" I howl.

A few yards away a sheaf of papers goes airborne as a startled Dennie upsets them. "Yes? Is there a problem?"

"Where did you get this offer?"

"From a man! With a very thick accent. He called and asked for me!"

Well, that seals it. Nobody ever calls and asks for Dennie. Braht is playing both of us for fools.

I shoot to my feet. This is some serious bullshit. And I'm going to get to the bottom of it. Keys in hand, I charge out the back door and jump into my car. It's not a long drive to Braht's house. And yet I manage to get even angrier on the way over there.

In the first place, Braht's big plan is preventing me from solving my own problems. This was supposed to be the moment when I paid back my parents for all the help they gave me when I was in trouble. I'm a big girl, damn it.

Furthermore—and more importantly—sneaking around is not how couples behave. How many times did Braht ask me to *trust* him? That's right—dozens. He said he was nothing like my ex. My lying, sneaking ex.

Is there no man on this whole fucking planet who isn't out to deceive me?

I am going to rip him a new one, because all it took to make this right was a simple conversation. *Hey, Ash, I have a plan that affects your family and your future. Let's discuss it together.*

How hard is that?

And then it hits me—an even worse scenario. Maybe Braht is not trying to help me at all. He said he loved the cottage. Maybe he actually wants it for himself. Or maybe he has a plan to flip it for profit.

In other words, Braht's offer on the cottage is either a dramatic romantic gesture, or a super-sleazy maneuver. It has to be one or the other.

My blood pressure is officially through the roof. So when I pull up in front of Casa Braht, I'm practically frothing at the mouth. I get out of the car and run up the walkway, flinging the front door open when I reach it. "Where are you, you sleazy snake?"

"If that's a sexual reference, please don't explain it," comes the answer. But it's not Braht's voice. It's Bramly's. A moment later he appears in the entryway, a granola bar in his hand and a camera around his neck. "Hello, Ash. If you're looking for my brother, he's not here."

"Oh." And now all my bluster has nowhere to go. "Will he be back soon?"

"No idea. I'm all done taking the photographs. Now I'm just raiding the fridge."

"Photographs?"

"For the listing. Braht liked my work on yours so much, he asked me to do his. The listing just went up this morning, so it's a rush job."

The listing. My blood pressure rises one more notch. "He put his house on the market," I say slowly.

Bramly puts a hand on the sleek wooden banister. "I'll miss this place. When I was sixteen, Sebastian bought it from a divorcing couple whose sale fell through. It was great to move back into a real house. Our apartment was so skanky those first few years." He shivers. "Anyway, Braht says he doesn't need all this room anymore since I've moved out."

My head is spinning now. I clutch the banister, too.

"Later." Bramly shrugs, oblivious to my confusion. "Gotta run. Lock up when you go?"

"Sure," I grunt.

He leaves a minute later, and I draw my phone out of my pocket and tap on Braht's name. He answers immediately, on speakerphone. He must be in his car, because I hear road noise. "*Sebastian Braht*. What the ever-loving fuck is going on with you? You are buying my parents' cottage? And you put your own house on the market?"

"Yes," he says after only the briefest pause. "I was going to tell you the whole thing tonight."

"HOW THOUGHTFUL!" I shriek. "You're sneaking around acting like a complete nut job, and I don't even get a phone call? How shady is that? Who does that?"

"You're right, Ash. It was shitty. I have a lot to tell you and I'm really sorry. There's so much I should have already said."

"Well, yeah." His outright apology slows me down. "So start talking."

"I will. I'm on my way home now. Can you come over in an hour?"

"Listen, dicknozzle. I'm standing in your living room right now with nothing better to do than to hear your explanation."

He sighs. "There's some kind of accident on the S-curve, and I'm stuck in traffic. I want to tell you all of this in person. And there's a potential buyer on his way to the house right now."

"This house?"

"Yes. Mine. I got some interest right after I listed it."

Figures. I put the cottage and my own house on the market and the only offers I get are from myself and Braht. He puts his house up and gets a call two seconds later. I hate him a little bit more.

"I hate you right now," I mutter.

He sighs. "I know, okay? But hold that thought a little longer. Could you please let in my buyer if he gets there before I do?"

My blood pressure goes shooting into previously uncharted territory. "Sure, hon! Let me just sell your house for you while you dodge my important questions!" My voice is echoing off Braht's elegant high ceilings. I'm so done with him right now.

"Listen. I know I'm an asshole of the most gaping proportions and I deserve every word of this," he says. "Especially since the last guy you trusted took your money and stole from your employer."

"Thank you!" At least I'm not the only witness to the universe's fuckery.

"I love you and I never meant to hurt you, and God willing I'll be there to say it in person within the half hour. But for the love of all that's holy I need to get off the phone and find an alternate route."

"Fine," I bite out. "But this is my client. If he buys your stupid house I get the commish."

He actually laughs. "I would have been disappointed if you didn't think to nail that down ahead of time."

Against all my better instincts, I smile. I feel both love and rage right now, and those two emotions are duking it out in my chest. "Just get here already." At that, I hang up on him. I really like getting the last word.

And then I go right into realtor mode, because even in a crisis, I'm still me.

Bramly left a few crumbs in the kitchen, and I quickly discard them. I start a pot of coffee brewing, because sixty-one percent of survey respondents exhibit a favorable emotional reaction to the scent of fresh coffee. It's one of my favorite tricks.

Upstairs, things are already tidy from Bramly's photo session. There are a couple of debauched-looking roses reclining on each bed, and a terry cloth robe hanging invitingly in the bathroom. To make the bathroom counter appear larger, I put away four different luxury face creams.

They all say "pour l'homme," but I roll my eyes anyway. Braht uses nicer cosmetics than I do.

I miss him so much it hurts.

Downstairs, someone knocks twice on the front door.

"Come in!" I yell from upstairs. I quickly finish up my work as I hear the door open and shut again.

Then I hear the bolt slide shut.

Okay, that's a little weird.

"Hello there!" I call. But nobody answers. And as I descend the stairs, no one is visible. Whoever just arrived has headed toward the kitchen.

"Hello?" I call. "Braht?" Did he make it home?

No response. But then I hear the back door lock, too.

That's when all the hair stands up on the back of my neck. Whoever I'm here with has just locked both doors. And now I hear footsteps treading slowly toward the living room, where I am now standing. "Hello!" I call one more time. "In here!"

Still, nobody returns my greeting. I feel the sudden, irrational urge to flee. Every female real estate agent has felt this way, though. Touring empty homes with unfamiliar men is just part of the job.

It's nothing, I tell myself.

And then the last man I want to see today steps through the doorway.

27 GOOD LUCK, SUCKER

Braht

This traffic is horrible.

I get off the expressway only to find that the roads are no better. There's construction on Wealthy Street and I'm inching along, waiting to get past the asphalt truck.

My stomach is full of acid. Ash is *pissed*. And I know it's only going to get worse.

That's when my phone starts pinging. And it's an alert I don't recognize.

"Siri," I grumble. "What the fuck is that notification?"

"Let me check on that, Braht," she says coolly. I love Siri's voice, I really do. It's half helpful and half *good luck, sucker*. Apparently I have a thing for smart, capable women who aren't always warm to me.

I wait. I inch my car up toward the next car's bumper, because eighteen inches of progress is going to make a big difference in my life.

"You have three alerts," Siri says. "Bands In Town would like you to know that a Pink Floyd tribute band is playing in your area on Saturday. You have a teeth whitening appointment tomorrow at ten a.m.. And the target of your tracking app has approached your home."

Wait, what?

I grab the phone off the dash and unlock it. I jab the PI's tracking app and wait for the map to resolve itself. The red dot—Dwight Engersoll—is heading through my own neighborhood, in the direction of my house.

Where Ash is waiting for me. "Holy fuck!"

"I didn't catch that," Siri says frostily.

The car ahead of me lurches forward maybe six feet and then stops again. Without even giving it a second thought, I use the extra space to pull off the road and onto the sidewalk. In what will be the closest I'll ever come to a *Dukes of Hazzard* car jump, I buck the curb, peel through a church parking lot and then back onto the road in front of an open-mouthed road crew.

Then I gun it.

Later I won't even be able to remember the next few minutes of driving. I basically go into ninja mode, my senses taking over while my brain is given over to panic.

The drive should have taken nine more minutes, but I do it in four.

Meanwhile, the app alert continues to bleat, and Siri continues to scare me shitless by announcing Dwight's progress at invading my home.

Beep beep. "The target is one kilometer away from Casa Braht." *Beep beep.* "The target is a half kilometer away." *Beep beep.* "A hundred meters." And then, "The target is circling the block. Now he has stopped his vehicle in front of your home."

Two minutes after that I roar into my own driveway, brakes squealing as I try not to crash into the back wall of my own garage. Mere seconds later I have my key in the back door. I get it unlocked, but the door won't open. Someone has jammed it shut from inside.

Heart pounding, I fly into the backyard and leap onto the

patio. Rambo himself would be proud as I drag a deck chair over to the kitchen window. This was Bramly's favorite way to get inside whenever he locked himself out as a teen. So I put both hands on the window sash and shove it upwards. Diving through, I clear the kitchen sink with a graceless tumble onto the floor below.

That will leave a bruise. But I'm on my feet already, listening. I hear pounding upstairs, and my heart leaps into my throat as the shouting starts.

"Just open the door, you crazy bitch! I'm not going to hurt you."

Gee, it's really a wonder that Dwight has done so well in life. So charming and persuasive...

These are my thoughts as I run full tilt up the stairs to rescue my girl.

Ash

I have barricaded myself in Braht's master bathroom, and I am steaming mad. And a little scared.

Fine—a lot scared. My hands are shaking as I stand here wielding...I don't know what this thing is. Some kind of manscaping tool. But it has shiny metallic teeth and it's the best idea I've had in the last ten seconds.

The moment I spotted Dwight downstairs, he began to talk. But I wasn't buying what he was selling. So I turned tail and ran upstairs into Braht's room and locked the door. Then onward into the bathroom, and I locked that door, too.

It didn't work, though. The kind of lock they put on bedroom doors is only meant to keep out curious children who might interrupt you in the middle of sex. It's not a lock for keeping out ex-con ex-husbands.

While I stand here hyperventilating, I hear him enter the

bedroom. He probably picked the lock. That's the kind of thing you learn in prison, right?

Holy shit, I'm going to die with a men's shaving tool in my hand. And I haven't even owned a pair of Louboutins, yet. *I'm not ready!*

Dwight snarls at me from outside the bathroom door. Trembling now, I turn away to investigate the bathroom window. Unfortunately, it looks out onto a particularly slippery bit of metal roof. If I'm forced to exit the premises that way, it's going to hurt. A lot.

"Just!" *Bang.* "Open!" *Bang.* "The fucking..." *Bang.* "Door!" Dwight shouts. "I need one stupid little thing, and you'll never see me again, you stuck-up bitch."

"Keep talking!" I yell. "It will give the police more time to respond to my 911 call!" My voice is shaking, though. Can he hear the lie?

"Your phone is in the front hall," he growls. "But if you listen for just one goddamn minute you know that all I need is..."

But I don't get to hear what he needs, because there's a sudden and mighty crash against the door, and I jump like a horror movie audience member.

Yet the door holds. And I hear... Is that the sound of fighting? The thumps and bumps are desperate and disorganized.

Dwight screams, and my lungs seize up completely.

"I would put you out of your misery right this second," a new voice says. It's Braht's! I feel the first hint of relief. "...Except prison food is too carby and I don't look good in orange."

My exhale is mighty.

"Get off me, you penny loafer-wearing pussy!" Dwight shouts, and I tense up again as I hear more flailing. But then Dwight makes a sick little wet sound and whimpers.

"That's right. You called it." Braht lets out a dark chuckle. "But *I'm* the penny loafer-wearing pussy who's got you pinned. Honey bear! Are you okay?"

"Y-yes," I squeak.

"Then bring me an electrical cord. Like the hair dryer, maybe, or—"

I yank open the bathroom door to find Dwight flat on the carpet, face down, his hands wrenched behind his back by Braht. "There's blood!" I whimper. It's all over Braht's hands.

"Oh, baby, it's okay. Bella will just have to be gentle at my next manicure. My knuckles are a little busted. Hand that over, okay?"

I look down and see that I'm still holding the shaving tool.

Braht takes it out of my hand and uses the cord to wrap up Dwight's wrists. Then he sits right down on Dwight's ass, which makes Dwight grunt with indignation.

"Wow." Braht lets out a breath. "First things first, I want a hello kiss."

"So do I," Dwight snarls.

Without even a glance at what he's doing, Braht smacks Dwight's exposed cheek. "Shut up. Quick now," he says to me. "A kiss, and then the cordless phone."

I'm rooted to this spot in the bathroom, though. It freaks me out to get close to Dwight. "In...a minute," I argue.

Braht makes a gentle clicking sound with his tongue. "The sooner you bring me that phone, the sooner he's out of our lives. You can bet that breaking and entering is a parole violation. You got this, Ash. The phone, please."

I'm still in a daze, but his voice is just the right amount of calm and demanding. So I step over Dwight's prone form and into the hallway where there's more room to avoid him. Then I turn and scamper into the bedroom to grab the phone.

When I return, Braht takes the phone in one hand and somehow dials 911 while holding Dwight. "Yes, this is an emergency. I need to report a break-in. The man who forcibly entered my home already has an outstanding arrest warrant."

He speaks calmly into the phone while I stand there feeling shaky. The fear just won't release its hold on me. When I saw Dwight walk into the room with me...

A shudder travels through my body. I can't even think about

that moment without wanting to cry. I thought he was going to kill me.

"Honey bear," Braht says softly. He's off the phone. "Come closer."

Reluctantly I kneel down beside him. He leans forward and kisses my forehead. It's just a little brush of his lips across my skin. But that tiny contact lets me feel things again. "I was so scared," I whisper. "I hate being scared!"

"It's going to be okay."

And he's right. The cops show up and ask us a lot of questions. Dwight argues that he didn't break in because he'd made an appointment to see Braht's house. But the busted bedroom door argues otherwise. Also, Dwight gave Braht a false name when he made the appointment.

When they search Dwight's pockets, the cops find a strange little device with a light on it. It looks like a pen, but it's a little too large.

"That is a spy camera!" Braht yelps. "Were you going to leave that in my *house?*"

At that thought, I shiver yet again. Braht tucks me against his side, and I try to relax against his warmth.

"You can't prove that," Dwight argues. "But if Ash would just answer a simple question then I could have left you alone."

"What. Question?" I bite out.

"Our, uh, wedding date."

I blink down at him, and then blink again. "Wait, *what?* You need to know what date we were married? Why?"

"Never mind why," he grumbles.

"Maybe it's a password," Braht suggests.

But my brain is still stuck back on wedding date. "How do you *not* know when we got married?" I demand. "It was your stupid idea."

"Well..." he chuckles nervously. "I remember that part."

"Oh MY GOD!" I'm getting angry again, and it feels good. It's better than cowering. "Men! You are unbelievable."

"Not all of us," Braht counters. "I happen to know that you married him on October 28th, 2011," Braht says.

"How do you know that?" Dwight demands.

"It was in the PI's file," Braht says to me.

"But I tried all the dates in October..." Dwight seems to catch himself, and he zips his lip.

"Tried them on *what?*" the cop asks, jotting down another note. "Is it the combination to something important?"

"Uh, never mind," Dwight says feebly.

"WAIT!" I exclaim, leaping to my feet. "Did you need that camera to look at my butt? My old tattoo..." It was our wedding anniversary date. Six digits.

Dwight bites his lip, careful not to say anything.

But Braht leaps to his feet, too. "Are you fucking *kidding* me right now? You were going to put a camera in my home so you could see Ash's ass?"

"Never said that," Dwight grunts.

"Nobody sees that ass but me!" Braht's face is red. He takes a step closer to the handcuffed Dwight and makes a fist.

The cop who's sitting with us grabs him. "Careful, buddy. I only want to take one of you downtown. He's neutralized. You can't hit him even if he deserves it."

"Can I hurl an expletive at him?"

The cop shrugs. "Sure."

"You are a fucking dweeb who needs to get his eyebrows done."

The cop laughs.

"Get him out of here," Braht says through clenched teeth.

"Jamison!" the cop calls to his partner in the other room. "Let's go, okay? And tell the detective to pull this guy's old case file. If there was missing cash somewhere he'll need a warrant to search for a combination safe."

"Got it!" Jamison says. "Let's take 'im downtown now and book 'im."

They haul the prisoner to his feet, one cop on either side. "I guess this is goodbye again," I say flatly to Dwight. I've earned this closure and I'm taking it. "Lose my number, okay? I spent too many years trying to undo the damage you caused."

He skulks out on the cop's arm, and I watch his backside disappear out Braht's front door. I've come a long way since I was the kind of girl who could be taken in by a dope like Dwight.

Braht

I have the kind of adrenaline rush that just won't quit. I feel like a goddamn superhero. I could scale the walls right now and swing by wrist-webs across the city.

Dwight is gone. Ash is safe from him.

She's in my kitchen, rustling around. And when she returns, it's with a bag of corn chips and a bowl of salsa. And two beers.

Have I mentioned that she's the perfect woman? Oh right, I have. And she's still going to leave me. "We have to talk," I say.

"No shit, Sherlock." She hands me a beer. "Or rip each other's clothes off. I'm so hyper right now I could go all day. My nipples are steel tipped right now." She covers her mouth with one hand. "Something is wrong with me if I just said that out loud."

"Tell them to chillax for a minute, because I have some things I need to get off my chest." You know shit is serious if I'm turning down sex with the love of my life. But I can't make love to her again unless she knows the whole ugly story.

"Promise me," she says, swigging her beer. "...That you wouldn't forget our wedding date. Who does that?"

Right? I can't even imagine. Marrying Ash would turn me into one of those guys who sobs through his own wedding vows. It wouldn't be a man card moment, that's for sure. "If I ever have the honor of marrying you, that date would be burned into my soul."

She gives me a soft smile, and I die a little inside. "There won't be any more tattoos on my ass. I think I jinxed myself."

"Nah. That dickhead did all the jinxing when he decided the world owed him a free paycheck."

Her smile widens. "You know what's funny? The tattoo artist was European. So he wrote the date..."

"In reverse order!" I cackle. "That's hilarious. So it said, 28-10-11?"

"Yup!" she shoves a chip in her mouth with obvious glee.

"That's why Dwight was traipsing around after you. He needed to crack the code. I wonder what he needs that code for?"

"It doesn't matter. I've spent too much time and effort on Dwight. Now I want to spend some time and effort on you. And you can spend more on *me*."

I take a quick look at her nipples. Still steel tipped. God, I want her. I bite my fist.

Yes, it's overly dramatic, but there are times in life that call for a good old fist-biting and this is one of them. "Ash, you know I love you."

"Yes," she says softly.

"But there's something I didn't tell you, and you're going to take it hard."

Her eyes widen. "Why?"

"Because..." I take a deep breath. "It's my fault your parents lost the cottage."

She tilts her head to the side like a confused puppy. "No, it's HIMCO's fault."

"HIMCO was my dad's company. He defrauded everyone and then left the country."

"He..." Her eyes widen. "And you're his...?" She gulps.

"Yes." I fill in the missing details, including my role in it. I talk for like five minutes straight while I pace and I scrub my hands through my hair.

It all feels very Romeo and Juliet and cursed.

"...And that's why I offered on the cottage for you. I'll sell my place and live in a shoebox somewhere and just get by. I want to do this even if you don't want to see me anymore."

"Braht! Shut up a second!"

I stop pacing, but it isn't easy because I was really on a roll.

"You dick bean! I'm not blaming you for your dad's bullshit, or something you didn't understand when you were just a kid."

"I was eighteen."

She waves a hand as if brushing away a mosquito. "Please. At eighteen I thought frosted lipstick was a good idea and that Christina Aguilera could see inside my soul. I forgive myself for my teen years, and you should, too."

It couldn't possibly be that easy. But that fact that Ash thinks so stuns me into silence for once in my life.

"...And if you think for a minute I'm letting you go after investing all this emotional trust in you, then you've got your head up your ass. I *love* you. Did you know that?"

I shake my head. Another bomb goes off inside my poor little brain.

"Well, I do. I love your pastel colors and your pedicures. I love that you're more high maintenance than I am and that I can bogart your moisturizer in the morning. I love that you exasperate me at work and you exhaust me in the bedroom. Of course we're going to be together. It's fucking obvious. I want to secure my rate of investment."

Now it's starting to get through, because she's speaking our common language. She wants a good ROI?

She wants a good ROI! From me! "Oh, honey bear. I love it when you talk business. Come here right now." I point at the floor in front of me. "I need to make a deposit on our mutual account."

Ash gives me a catty look. "Will I get a good return?"

"Off the charts," I whisper.

She takes a step closer, and I just want to kiss her. Like, yesterday. So I close the distance and crush my mouth over hers.

Soft arms tight around me, and she moans into my mouth. I can't believe my luck. Ash and I make sense, damn it. And she's one thing my parents didn't actually steal away.

She breaks our kiss. "Now take off your clothes and let me see your mighty braht, *Sebastian*."

My mighty braht. I like that. "On the bed, hot stuff."

She races toward my room, and I'm in hot pursuit. Very hot. Because forgiveness makes me horny.

But then, when she's just three feet from the bed, Ash comes to a halt. She stops so fast that I run into her, my hard cock poking her right in the ass.

"*Ungh*," I say, when I really mean, "whoops, sorry."

She turns around slowly, and I spot her wide eyes. "Braht," she whispers.

"Yes, sexy thing?" The bratwurst is ready to party, so I unzip my khakis.

"What does HIMCO stand for?"

"Um..." I shed my pants. I'm so hard I've literally forgotten my own name. Or rather, my father's. "Hunter Investment Management Company."

"*Hunter*," she squeaks. "Omigod."

"You can say that, baby, but preferably when I'm inside you." I reach out and begin unbuttoning her blouse.

She puts a hand on my chest. "Your real name is Hunter."

"It was." But that was a long time ago.

"My fake boyfriend is Hunter."

"Don't talk about other dudes when we're getting naked, baby." I unhook her bra and let those titties free. The nipples aim right at me, like a well-calibrated missile system.

I lean over to take one of them in my mouth.

"Oh fuck," she gasps. "That feels...ungh. But...I'm having a revelation here."

"Yeah?" I push her down on the bed. "Can you have it while I'm licking you everywhere?"

"Sebastian!" She grabs my head in two hands so that I'll pay attention. "Listen. My subconscious is such an asshole."

"I know, baby." So is mine, though, because my subconscious insists on thinking about sex with Ash even while she's trying to talk to me.

"I named my fake boyfriend Hunter. On some level I already think I knew it was you."

"Mmm." This has occurred to me before. I just really need to hear her say it. "Really?"

"Really. I don't know why I fought you for so long."

"Me either, sugar pop. How about we declare a truce and I pound you into the mattress now?"

"Okay," she sighs, reclining on the bed. "Carry on, good sir."

So I spread myself out on top of her and kiss her senseless. Because this is what you do when your soul mate finally accepts you. You kiss her and then make love to her until you both see stars.

Or until you both need to stop for a shower, some luxury bath products and a latte.

28 EPILOGUE

Ash

The snow has blanketed everything in white. And I mean everything. When you're on a lake in Michigan, that shit does not mess around. It's a Winterpocalypse out there.

I like snowstorms, at least lately. Braht and I are wearing ridiculously cozy sweaters—cashmere, not Christmas sweaters—joggers and slippers. The fire is crackling and he's got my dad's record player going. He also has a pork roast cooking. For tacos. It turns out Braht can cook exactly two things: tacos and omelets.

So yeah. He's pretty much perfect.

I peek outside again. It's like looking at a snow globe that's just been swirled. "They're not going to make it!" I cry.

Braht harrumphs. "They're going to make it."

"The roads are probably hazardous. They should just stay home."

"While the idea of feeding you tacos, naked, by the fire is really tempting, I gotta tell you, they'll be here. Tom has a very macho truck. It practically revs testosterone."

As if on cue, I hear the *grrr* of a massive engine.

I can't see anything, but it's okay. I know they've arrived. My

233

besties and Tom are here, and there will be piles of food and wine, because Brynn and Sadie would never show up empty handed.

"They made it!" I cry and open the door. Then I immediately shut it because that shit is cold.

A couple of minutes later, the door opens again, and gusts of icy air and snow swirl inside, along with packages and ham and hugs and mittens and whatever. I half expect Tiny Tim to limp by carrying an enormous turkey.

"That was crazy!" Brynn cries.

"I was saying a silent prayer to Gaia on that last hill," Sadie says.

I don't know how to respond to that, so I just open my arms and the three of us hug. Our scents drift together: chocolate, clove, and Candy Kiss by Prada. We are warm and soft and I'm not crying. I'm not. I've got something in my eye.

"I brought booze!" Tom says. "And sparkling grape juice, for whoever is underage or preggers!"

Brynn is not pleased with her beverage choices, but the rest of us are super excited. When I turn to kiss Tom hello, at first glance I think he's pregnant, too. But then I notice that it's only that he's wearing both of Sadie's babies. They're not exactly babies anymore, they're more like little...people.

I stare at Amy and Kate. "Hello," I say.

"Bullshit!" one of them says. And she says it with a lot of gusto.

I'm totally impressed. "Hand that one over," I demand. He gets to work undoing the complicated buckle/pulley system that's holding them, and I scoop the one who curses off the floor and snuggle her.

This is the best house party ever, even if Mom and Dad aren't here. They're visiting relatives in Canada and trying to decide on their retirement plan. If they move north, I will miss them. But they might not. The capital they got from selling me the cottage gives them more choices than they had before.

I closed on this place only a week ago, after my little house on the bike trail sold to a couple of yuppie accountants. It's someone else's starter home now.

And as for me? I've moved in with my man.

Braht wouldn't hear of me looking for a little studio of my own. "I know it's kind of soon," he said. "But I want you with me."

"Maybe it isn't too soon," I'd said. "I know you. I love you. I finally got it right this time."

Then I let him tie me to the bed with Hermès neckties and it was glorious.

We are very happy in his house together, but I wanted to have a holiday party here at the cottage. It's the start of a new era. I'm home with Braht and my friends. And it's nearly Christmas.

The men get cooking in the kitchen, while the kids are set up with playdough in the corner. That's when Brynn, Sadie, and I retreat to the living room to snuggle up on the couch and chat.

I bring them up to speed on Dwight. He's in prison again and it doesn't seem like he'll be out anytime soon. "He had a safe in his sister's basement, full of cash. They traced the serial numbers on the bills back to a scam he was running before he even met me."

"What a *dick*," Brynn says.

"Dick!" one of the twins yells.

Whoops.

Brynn tells us that she's in her second trimester now and feeling loads better. She has the cutest little pooch of a belly. Her cooking show episodes are done for the season, and she's racked up a few sponsors.

It seems like Brynn might be the next TV star in her family, with Tom helping behind the scenes. She seems really happy.

Sadie...Sadie is another story. "I'm fine!" she assures us. "The girls are doing well. Decker is paying extra child support because I have more custodial days than he does. And I just got two spots at the Small Packages daycare. It'll give the girls time to socialize and time for me to focus on the health of my clients."

Everything she's saying is positive, but... "What the fuck, Sadie?"

There's a bit of a pause, then Brynn chimes in: "Yep. What. The. Fuck. The girls are good. Your ex is fine. Your clients are doing well. But where are you?"

"What do you mean where am I? I'm right here! I'm fine."

"You're fine," I say. "But you're miserable. You're usually all glowy. Now you're sort of matte."

"Yep," Brynn agrees. "Definitely a matte finish. No shine."

I slap my knee. "You know what you need?"

"What?" Her response does not express excitement. Then again I'm known for telling my friends what to do. But only because I'm right.

"You need a boy toy! Hot sex and relaxation!"

Brynn shakes her head. "Oh no. She doesn't need a boy toy."

"*Thank* you," Sadie says. "I'm doing fine by myself."

"What I meant was—" Brynn clarifies"—that she needs a *man* toy."

"Oh my god!! A man toy! Yes!" Brynn and I high-five over Sadie's head.

"I don't need anything of the kind," she grumbles. But I see the tiniest bit of blush to her cheeks.

She may not think she needs one, but she wants one. I can tell.

Braht

The next night, after everyone has left, the snow is really swirling. We may have to stay up here at the cottage for a few days, and that's just fine with me. I decide to give her an early Christmas present. "I have something for you," I say, "But I need to change into my bathrobe first."

"Uhm..." she says. "If you need some help undressing, I'm totally here for that."

That's super appealing, but I tell her to be patient. "Actually, why don't you make yourself more comfortable in front of the fire?"

Her eyes sparkle with amusement. "I think I will."

"Here we go!" When I return a couple of minutes later, my hands are full. "Three gifts."

Her eyes narrow. "I see two?"

"You'll understand in a second. Here." I hand over the larger, squishy one.

She gives me a happy smile and then tears the paper off. "Oh my god. This is hilarious." She's smiling at the rug I just gave her, and it's smiling back. It's a faux bearskin, complete with a stuffed animal head.

"That goes right here," I say, pointing to the floor in front of the fireplace.

"*Really*," she says with a smirk. "Whatever would we do there?"

"Tough call, really," I say. "But before you work it out, open this." I hand her a slim little package.

"It's obviously a book," she says, smiling down at the wrapping paper. "Let me guess. The complete collection of Naked Braht, photography by Bramly Hunter?"

"I'm saving that for Christmas morning," I tell her. "Open it."

She tears off the paper and gasps. "Omigod. It's perfect."

I've bought my girl a new planner—a luxury, personalized version. The cover reads: "Ash-kicker's Plan for World Domination."

She lets out a happy squeak and opens the cover, then proceeds to fondle the pages. "Ooh! A section for goals and lists. Nice paper weight. Great layout! I love it." She flips forward to where the calendar starts. "Thank you for not writing *hot sex with Braht* on every page. I need to be able to open this in public."

"Pfft." I wave a dismissive hand. "That's just understood. I wouldn't write *breathe in and out* in a planner, either."

But speaking of hot sex. I reach into my bathrobe and give

myself a slow, happy stroke. "It's time for your third gift." I part the two halves of my robe, giving her a nice look at my braht tied with a shiny, satin bow on.

"You did not!" she says, clapping her hands over her mouth. "You put a bow on your dick!"

"I thought putting it in a box was a little creepy."

She laughs until she almost can't breathe. I use this time to kiss her neck. And then the laughter stops, and the moans begin. I remove her clothes and toss the bear rug on the floor.

There is still a bow on my erection.

"Come here," she says in my favorite bossy voice. "It's just what I wanted." We roll around on the bear, kissing, until Ash says, "Bring me my purse."

"What?"

"My bag. I need it."

"I think you need something else instead, baby." I tongue her nipple.

"Patience." She pushes my face away with the heel of her hand. God, I love her. "You're not getting any until I get to give you a gift."

Since she means business, I sit up and find the damned bag and hand it over.

"Thank you. I got you two things." She rifles through the purse.

"One"—I touch her breast—"two"—I touch the other...

She bats my hand away. "Two *other* things. Here's the first one." She hands me a tiny envelope, taped shut with that cute designer tape that she orders from Korea. When I open it, there's a metal card inside.

"MAN CARD" is engraved on the front. Then, in small letters, *Can never be revoked.*

"Aw!" It's the coolest. "Can I keep it even if I make you watch *Love Actually* again tonight?"

"You can," she admits. "The minute you stood up for me, I knew you were the real deal."

"Oh, honey bear. I need to celebrate by…"

She holds up a hand before I can say, *boink you on the floor now.* "One more." She reaches into the bag and pulls out another little envelope.

When I open this one, I'm really surprised. It's a business card. A real one. And it isn't like those crafty ones she carries, proclaiming her expertise in everything.

It's even cooler. It reads, *Ash Power & Sebastian Hunter Braht Realty.*

"Wow." It's a big idea. I love it already. "You know, we could shorten that to Power Braht Realty," I say.

"Oh my fucking God," she says. "We could! But does that sound dirty? Or is it just my nakedness talking?"

Her nakedness is talking, all right. It's shouting, even. "I love it. And I love you. And your nakedness. We'll figure it out later."

Ash doesn't bother agreeing with me. She just reaches down and takes me in her mouth.

I let out a not-so-manly gasp of surprise and delight.

The snow falls. Music plays. And I make sweet, sweet Power Braht love to my girl. Hopefully there's a real blizzard outside so we can just stay here for a while, cocooned from the world. I'll worship her every minute I can, for as long as she'll let me, because that's what a real man does with his lady love. He worships her.

I'm starting for real, right now.

Thank you for reading Man Card! We hope you enjoyed it. If so, you might consider leaving us a review. We really appreciate those!
And don't miss Man Hands, Brynn and Tom's book!

9 781942 444527